ADVERSE EVENTS

JJ Renek

Also by JJ Renek

Payoff

Seen & Unseen

NOTE: this novel is free of AI generated or revised content. No portion was written, edited, or enhanced through the use of AI.

- JJ Renck

This is a work of fiction. Names, places, characters and incidents are either the product of the author's imagination or are used fictitiously, and any resemblance to any actual persons, living or dead, businesses, organizations, events or locales is entirely coincidental.

No part of this book may be reproduced or transmitted in any form or by any means, electronic or mechanical, including photocopying, recording, or by any information storage and retrieval system, without permission in writing from the author.

Cover Design – Jaycee DeLorenzo
Publishing Coordinator – Sharon Kizziah-Holmes

Copyright © 2025 – Lakepoint Press LLC
All cover art copyright © 2025 – Lakepoint Press LLC
All Rights Reserved

Published by

LAKEPOINT PRESS LLC®

Paperback ISBN 13: 979-8-9905504-6-9
Hardcover ISBN 13: 979-8-9905504-7-6
eBook ISBN 13: 979-8-9905504-8-3

For Lisa

ONE

September 2019

Saturday

Being a Saturday, it was not a usual workday for Rachel Quinn. At least not so for the past couple of years. She depressed the doorbell and waited. Why had she agreed to this appointment, anyway?

Standing there on the small front porch, a metal awning overhead, she glanced at the large picture window to her right. No doubt the living room. Though the house faced east, the drapes were still drawn, apparently against the too harsh sun of Indian summer, which had passed overhead several hours before. In fact, she noticed the drapes were also drawn across the smaller window to the right of the living room. Likely a bedroom.

Multiple large trees shaded the entire property, their branches swaying in the warm wind. The garage doors to her left were closed, no sign of a car present on the property, although several discarded tires lay askew nearby. The red brick ranch, typical of that area, was a product of the building boom of the fifties and early sixties. This was truly a suburban area, far from the annoyances of the city and traffic, hard to find without exact directions. Most of the homes she had passed on the way there sat on small acreages, off poorly marked roads.

She pushed the bell and asked herself again why she'd agreed to this particular time. Usually, these one-on-one teaching sessions were scheduled and kept during regular weekday hours. And, yes, she tried to accommodate individuals with conflicting schedules who needed her services. But this situation felt like the proverbial run around—scheduling an appointment then no-showing. Still, she shouldn't complain. The teaching company allowed their independent contractors, nurses such as herself, to set their own schedules and meet with patients when it was mutually agreeable. So, she had better erase such thoughts and assumptions. This woman needed the proper information and instruction, not her irritation and consternation.

Rachel pushed the doorbell once more, holding it down a second longer. Silence followed—no TV, no music, no footsteps, no doors closing. Maybe the client was indisposed and couldn't make it to the door? Maybe she just wasn't there.

Her estranged husband Bill had seemed nice enough when Rachel dropped by his Olathe apartment—well, made the trek of fifteen extra miles to his apartment—to pick up the medication. For some reason, the patient had left it there when she last visited him. The explanation he'd given didn't exactly ring true.

He'd welcomed Rachel in, fetched the small, sealed package, and confessed he still cared deeply for his wife and hoped she could learn how to use the medication properly. He'd worried about her since she'd left. He hoped, maybe someday, she'd come to her senses, and they'd get back together again. And he appreciated all the extra effort Rachel was making to follow their rather convoluted directions that day. He had made sure she knew how to find Linda at her mother's home where she was camped out, on the other side of town, outside Kansas City, across the state line in Missouri. They'd said their goodbyes and Rachel departed, driving another thirty-five miles to reach the patient's present location in Peculiar, Missouri.

Was she, or anyone, ever going to come to the door? Frustrated, Rachel pressed the bell one last time, determined to leave if it wasn't answered in the next several minutes.

Suddenly, the door flew open. There stood a disheveled woman, appearing every day of her forty-nine years, brunette hair hanging limp below her shoulders, wearing knit pants with true knee definition and a tie-dyed tee shirt, and sporting sunglasses against the mid-afternoon sun. It was apparently lost on her that she faced east, and that the tree shade effectively cut any direct sun on the house. A sun which would be totally obscured before too many hours passed by gathering thunderheads in the west.

"Oh, you're here," she said, greeting Rachel. "Do you have the drug?"

"Yes, I'm Rachel Quinn, the nurse educator. You must be Linda Bates."

"Yeah, that's me. Come on in." Linda turned and walked away into the dark interior, leaving Rachel to let herself in.

After passing into the small entry, she removed her own sunglasses and instinctively left the front door ajar. Given the circumstances, it seemed the prudent thing to do. The stench of stale cigarettes hit her. One risk factor for sure—smoking.

While her eyes adjusted to the relative darkness, Rachel glanced around. She took a few cautious steps forward onto the worn green carpet and noted that newspapers and magazines, trash bags, and various other detritus covered nearly all surfaces, including the upholstered furniture. A large-screen TV occupied one corner of the room, thankfully turned off. Two half-cocked recliners sat positioned for best viewing, not six feet away from the massive TV.

Adjacent to the small living room, Rachel noted a dining room furnished with a vintage maple table, six chairs gathered haphazardly around it. Drapes drawn, as well. The tabletop was covered with various placemats, used dishes, several pots and pans, a dish of what looked like pet food, more newspapers, a hairbrush, toothbrush, and a twisted tube of toothpaste. Apparently, the strategic location from which day-to-day life was conducted. There was no place to position her laptop and teach this woman anything about the prescribed medication.

Out of the corner of her eye, Rachel detected movement and turned slightly. A large brindle cat materialized, and crept toward the table, obviously interested in the waiting pet food. She hoped she wasn't threatening his feeding territory. The huge cat looked capable of inflicting harm if it chose to launch onto a visitor or an intruder. Perhaps a Maine Coon Cat? Who cares what breed, she told herself, just steer clear if possible. Nonchalantly he slinked under the table.

Apparently noting Rachel's appraising look, Linda announced, "This is my mother's place. I'm only staying here. And that's Jack."

Not planning to converse with the big cat, Rachel ignored the introduction and asked, "Would she like to join us?"

"Mother, or Jack?"

"Your mother."

"No, she's in Las Vegas."

"I see. So, is there a place where I can set up my computer?" Rachel asked.

"Sure. Wherever you want."

Impatient then, Rachel gestured toward the living room, and suggested, "Why don't we make a place on your coffee table?"

Without answering, Linda walked toward a large brown rolled-arm couch and brushed aside the collection of materials lying there, providing a place to sit. Rachel followed her into the room, perched on the edge of the sofa, avoiding as much cat hair as possible, and turned toward Linda. It was time to take charge of this situation. While keeping an eye, of course, on Jack.

"May I?" she asked, gently moving aside the items, including a full ashtray, which covered the coffee table. Without waiting for further invitation, she placed her laptop on the table and pulled up the education company's website and the prepared slideshow. By God, she was going to do her best to get this woman instructed and get this over with.

While Rachel arranged her materials, Linda walked to the front door and shut it. "I want the door closed. The light bothers my eyes."

Risk factor number two—lack of exposure to sunlight. Or apparently any natural light. Rachel made a mental note to check with the medical office regarding this woman's vitamin D level, which she knew Dr. Reynolds had obtained. And give them feedback regarding Linda's aversion to daylight, just for the record.

"Okay, but I'll need a lamp on so I can see what I'm doing." Rachel went on, "I think you'll want to remove your sunglasses so you can view the screen better. And I also have a brochure for you to look over."

Surprisingly, Linda complied without protest.

Rachel began. "I went by your husband's—"

"He okay?"

"He seemed fine. I picked up the medication you left there. Had you tried it?"

"No, I was waiting for you to show up."

"Right. You know Dr. Reynolds has prescribed this for your osteoporosis, correct?"

"Yeah, that's what she said…my weak bones. I had that test and all."

Jack slinked by, rubbed against the table leg, and found a spot he seemed to prefer in the middle of the room. He sat straight up and stared at the two of them, his generous tail swishing with interest.

"Correct. It's been found that when your bone density is low enough to indicate osteoporosis, medications such as OAinvar actually help restore your bones' strength over time. It may keep you from having a fracture."

"You mean like breaking my rear?"

"Well, yes, your hip or wrist more likely." Rachel cleared her throat and went on. "Once you're taught, you can give yourself the weekly injection. You'll follow up with Dr. Reynolds regularly and they'll check your bone densities, as well as how you're tolerating the medication. If you have any questions about how to use it, after I go over this and you give yourself the first shot, you can call me. If you have problems with side effects, you'll need to call her office."

"What kind of side effects?"

"I'll go over that as we go through this information."

"I usually have lots of effects to any medicines I take. I don't want this to make me sick."

"It's tolerated very well, and most people have no problems. But I'll review the things to watch for, and to call her office about. Shall we start?"

Linda sat silent and Rachel seized the moment, clicking on the first slide in her presentation. Progressing through the first portion of the material explaining osteoporosis and the development of drugs to treat it, Linda appeared to pay attention to the slides, offering no objections nor questions. As slide eight scrolled onto the screen, showing the pre-loaded syringe and tiny 30-gauge,

3/16-inch needle, Linda abruptly threw herself back against the sofa cushions and exclaimed, "I can't shoot myself with some needle like that. I hate needles." She covered her eyes with one arm.

This was a first—the drama, not the stated aversion to needles. Rachel stopped the slide show and regarded Linda. Hearing nothing further, she pressed on and reassured her, "Many patients feel that way at first. But, after they practice, they realize it's no problem. The needle is so fine and small. There's very little, really no, pain associated with the injection. Most people say they don't even feel it. It's quite easy to get used to." She refrained from adding, 'and if you need reading glasses you probably can't even see it without them.'

Linda flung her arm down. "Well, I'm a very sensitive person, and everything like that bothers me."

"I understand." After a moment, Rachel went on, "Okay, why don't we keep going and I think it will seem easier when we finish."

Saying nothing, Linda remained cradled against the sofa cushions as Rachel forged ahead. No stranger to patient protests regarding self-injection, she felt confident she could convince Linda to try the medication at least once. True, this patient and her declarations were not exactly typical of her usual patients, but she'd had nothing but success in the past. Somehow this would work, too. And if it didn't, well, chalk it up to experience and move on. Linda could return to Dr. Reynolds for alternative treatments.

She continued through the remainder of the slides which illustrated injection preparation and administration, patients smiling and looking relaxed before and after they took the medication, and typical packaging of the drug. She then came to the slide with the usual side effects list.

Linda bolted forward and asked, "Are those all the things that can happen?"

"Yes," Rachel answered evenly, "these symptoms have been reported in some people who've taken the medication…a large group of patients who were given the medication during studies done before it was released to the market. Not everyone who takes it will experience all these side effects. In fact, since its release, serious side effects have not been a problem for the vast majority of people."

Staring at Rachel's computer screen, Linda recited the list of possible adverse reactions. "Nausea, dizziness, blurred vision, headache, shortness of breath, abdominal pain, joint pain, numbness in the extremities…what's extremities?"

"Your arms and legs."

Linda went on, "…feeling faint, bone pain, trouble urinating, constipation, diarrhea…what doesn't it cause?"

"The FDA requires each company to publish a list of any side effects that have ever been reported, particularly during the early studies and since its approval. All drugs that are released have a similar list of adverse effects or side effects. Again, that doesn't mean that a person will experience any, or all, of those symptoms."

She looked at Linda, and pointed at the screen. "If you'll notice below, it says less than ten percent of patients experience any of these side effects. The most common are these three, and they occur in about seven percent of patients."

"Well, I don't want any of that."

"Of course not."

"So, I don't think I can take this drug. My bones will just have to stay weak."

"It's certainly your choice. Do you want to stop now, or shall we go on?"

"I just can't give myself a shot if it's going to cause all that."

"Okay, Linda. That's fine." Thank heaven, she might be able to get out of there sooner. This wasn't going anywhere, fast. "I'll pack up and be on my way, and I'll let Dr. Reynolds' office know you don't want to give yourself a shot."

"Isn't there a pill I can take?" Before Rachel could inform her there wasn't, Linda whined, "Will she be mad at me?"

Collecting her laptop and associated paperwork, Rachel calmly stated, "No, there isn't a pill form of this drug, and no she won't be mad." She stood and turned toward Linda hoping to take her leave.

Linda shot off the sofa, took two steps, abruptly turned toward the dining room, and quickly pivoted again toward Rachel.

"I know I should do this but I'm so scared…oh, okay, I'll try it."

"Are you sure? We can do this another time. Perhaps if you come to Dr. Reynolds' office, we could try the medication there under her watchful eye."

"No, let's just get it over with."

Reluctant now, and half hoping Linda would decline again, Rachel put her messenger bag down on a chair near the front door. Pulling out the plastic medication sack, and her cell phone, she returned to the sofa and sat. Apparently settled down for the moment, Linda joined her there.

Rachel showed Linda the drug, explained the packaging and how to prepare the pre-loaded syringe for the one-time injection. She illustrated with the dummy syringe how to perform the injection, letting Linda practice on the small model. Linda appeared more comfortable as she practiced. It was time, then, for the actual injection. Rachel turned and faced her directly.

"Are you okay with giving yourself the shot now?"

"We'll see."

"We can wait."

"No, I'll do it now."

Rachel watched as Linda pulled her sweatpants off her right hip exposing her upper thigh, unsheathed the OAinvar, and prepared the skin area of her leg. With the syringe poised over her chosen site, she gave Rachel one last look, and stuck the needle in her leg. Frowning, she quickly removed it and dropped the entire uncapped syringe with needle on the couch. Rachel swept it up, recapped, and held it.

"So, that went well, and you did fine."

Rachel rose to fetch her satchel, intending to safely remove the spent syringe from the premises. Before she turned back to Linda, the woman complained, "I feel dizzy."

Pivoting, Rachel said, "Why don't you just rest right there? Usually, it's temporary and passes quickly. Perhaps you feel that way because you just gave yourself a shot."

As Linda swung around, throwing herself against the arm of the sofa, she exclaimed, "No, I'm having a reaction!"

Rachel returned to her side, swiftly grasped her wrist and took a pulse—eighty-four, and regular. "Your pulse is normal. Take easy breaths now. The dizzy feeling will likely ease. Just rest and I'll check your blood pressure."

Retrieving her blood pressure cuff and stethoscope from her bag, she again returned to Linda's side.

Hyperventilating, Linda complained, "I can't breathe. Something's wrong. I can't take that medication. I can't breathe," she panted.

Encompassing her upper arm with the blood pressure cuff, Rachel tried to calm the woman. *This is definitely spiraling out of control.* "Slow your breathing. That's why you feel short of breath and dizzy. You're hyperventilating."

Linda screamed, "I am not hyperbentilating! I'm having a reaction!"

It certainly was a reaction, true, but most likely not due to the medication. Managing to get the blood pressure taken—normal at 124/74—Rachel stood and stepped back from the couch, before Linda pushed up from her reclined position and announced she had to go to the bathroom, that she was 'going to have diarrhea any minute now.'

"I think you should stay put and give it a few minutes. That sensation should pass."

"No, I'm going to my bathroom. You don't know!"

With that she rolled off the couch, onto all fours, and crawled toward the bathroom in the hall, the blood pressure cuff still dangling from her arm. Aghast, Rachel stood in place debating whether to just leave the whole scene or follow the woman down the hall. Wisely, she opted for the latter. Once in the bathroom, she assisted Linda onto the toilet, confirmed she could sit upright then withdrew, instructing her she would wait outside the door just in case she needed her.

Leaning against the wall in the small hall, she took a deep breath and sighed. When would this end?

Two

Not soon enough. From outside the bathroom, hearing Linda moan and sigh and talk to herself, Rachel quickly made notes of the woman's pulse and blood pressure assessments, and her stated side effects. She risked leaving her position for a few moments to hurriedly retrieve her bag. Once again standing outside the bathroom door, she quickly repacked her papers while calling to Linda. "Are you doing all right?" No answer. She certainly hadn't heard any sounds suggestive of Linda hitting the floor. She waited.

After a few moments, she asked, "Linda, are you all right in there?" No answer.

Opening the door, she wasn't all together surprised to see the woman lying sprawled on the bathroom floor, her right arm draped over her eyes.

Rachel knelt by her side. "Linda, open your eyes."

Her eyes clamped shut, Linda demanded, "Call the paramedics. I need to go to the hospital. I can't see!"

"Linda, open your eyes." The woman cracked open one eye, then clamped it shut again. Rachel informed her, "And, no, you don't need to go to the hospital for this. Are you having pain?"

Linda refused to answer. Noting no flushing nor rash, Rachel quickly assessed the woman's pulse again. Normal. Blood pressure 130/80—normal. Her breathing was shallow and rapid, but not labored, no wheezing. Random movements confirmed she could move all extremities. And she certainly hadn't been rendered mute.

"I'm going to die. Call the paramedics."

"Why don't I help you up, and you can rest in bed for a while."

Linda screamed, "Call the paramedics! I'm dying…I want to go in!"

Rachel rose, and spoke in an even tone, "Just lay right there." At least she couldn't fall from her present position.

She retreated to the living room, leaving the bathroom door open. She could easily hear Linda repeatedly demanding she call the EMTs now, while also invoking the aid of the Almighty. Pulling out her cell phone, Rachel dialed 911. This had mushroomed into one ridiculous situation. She felt embarrassed pulling the paramedics in on such a scene. Perhaps she should have convinced the patient that she could drive her to the ER, though she wasn't sure she could safely drag Linda to her car, nor tolerate the drama and hysterics while in route.

Not ten minutes later the doorbell rang. Opening the front door, relief washed over her at the sight of two husky young men adorned in firemen's britches who stood there, smiling. She opened the door wider to admit them.

The two stepped inside. "You have an emergency here, ma'am?"

"No, I don't believe so, actually."

Smirking, they waited for an explanation.

She obliged with, "I'm Rachel Quinn, a nurse educator. I came here to teach Linda, Mrs. Bates, how to give herself the injectable medication OAinvar."

"What's it for?"

"Osteoporosis. When we went over the side effects, she had doubts. Well, since she gave herself the first injection she's complained of all known listed symptoms."

"Where's the patient, ma'am?" one asked.

"She's in her bathroom, lying on the floor."

"Passed out?"

"No, just lying there because she apparently wants to. Her blood pressure and pulse are normal. She's hyperventilating. No flushing or rash. She can move all extremities."

One paramedic broke away and went to the bathroom. Rachel

pulled out printed material on the medication and the known side effects, handing it to the second paramedic.

Glancing over it quickly, he asked, "May I take this with us?"

"Sure, no problem."

He smiled, and said, "We've been out here many times before. Linda's a frequent flyer. She calls all the time. Or her mother June Atwood does. Where's she?"

"Apparently in Las Vegas."

"Right." Smiling again and stuffing the wadded-up package insert in his pocket, he turned toward the bedroom hall. "Let's get rolling."

THREE

The garage door descended as the first flash of lightning split the sky, followed too soon by crashing thunder. Rather close in her estimation. Rachel expelled a slow sigh, very relieved to finally be back home. Back in her snug subdivision of patio homes, clustered behind a brick wall. And a large iron security gate.

Bundling her heavy messenger bag from the car and through the back door demanded all the remaining strength she possessed. Finding a nearby bar stool, she deposited her cargo. Thank goodness she'd taken her run early that morning. Her energy reserves were tapped out, and the approaching storm wouldn't permit outdoor exercise, anyway.

To say she was exasperated was an understatement. After assessing Linda on the bathroom floor, and despite her protestations that they couldn't move her or she'd die, the paramedics managed to hoist her onto their narrow gurney and mobilize her into their van. They had obtained all the necessary information Rachel could give them and bid her farewell, confident their patient would make it to the ER without further incident. No light or siren for that run. As a courtesy, while they loaded Linda, Rachel had checked on Jack's food and water, insuring he had sufficient provisions to get through that night and the next day. She'd even glanced at the litter box and decided Jack could stand it until Linda returned. Enough was enough. That really would go beyond the call of duty. As they'd all exited, she'd made sure the house was securely locked and, with a friendly wave, handed Linda her key. But, while driving home, she'd felt a twinge of guilt, reconsidered her exasperated mood, and decided she might give Linda's husband a quick call alerting him to check on the feline the next day. That would do it.

It was the most astounding teaching experience Rachel had ever had, including those times when an occasional nursing student hit the floor during a delivery or while learning to start an IV. This would definitely take extra time on Advanced Education Concepts' website to enter her visit data, and the plethora of adverse reactions the patient had experienced. Well, 'complained of' was a better way of putting it. Considering the time involved, she wisely decided to fix a little dinner before tackling the job.

Glad now she'd cleaned the day before, she flipped a switch and warm light bathed her kitchen. It struck her then how empty her kitchen looked compared to Linda Bates' environs. *Amazing.* The lights flickered once. No sooner had she made it to her refrigerator to search for dinner options than the lights flickered again, then extinguished, and she stood staring into her fridge's darkened interior. *Now what?*

Meanwhile, the storm raged. At her window then, she peered through the plantation shutters and watched rain sheet off the roof and overflowing gutters. Water pounded three cement pots holding newly planted chrysanthemums, discharging mud and plant parts all over the brick patio. What a mess. And she had just potted them yesterday.

Turning the shutters downward, she tapped her cell and brought up a local weather app. A big red radar blob sat directly over her area. The National Weather Service advised there was a severe thunderstorm in the area, moving at thirty-five mph, which should clear the vicinity altogether within the next forty-five minutes. Good. She could eat and probably still get her data entry done that evening.

Only five minutes passed before she heard the refrigerator hum again. Lights flickered once and relit the kitchen. She flipped another switch and the under-cabinet lights popped on, reflecting off the granite countertop. The nice clean sweep of countertop. She still couldn't decide what she felt like having, so instead of standing there, she retrieved her heavy messenger bag and headed down the back hall toward her bedroom and office. A change into more comfortable clothes was now the priority. It might help her settle down from the arduous afternoon, then she could face her evening.

From inside her walk-in closet, she heard her cell chime and decided to ignore it for the moment. If they had anything important to say, they could leave a message. And it was doubtful it was either her son or daughter. Heavens, they'd never think of calling their mother on a Saturday evening. But was it the ER calling about Linda?

Once changed and on her way back to the kitchen, she checked the number. It looked familiar but bore no caller ID. Definitely not the ER, though. She'd attend to it later, but now she should get about the business of eating, and drinking, if it came to that. With food and a glass of wine, her data entry from the home visit would likely go better than expected.

Later, at her desk with wine glass in hand, she started her computer and waited. Her paperwork and scribbled visit notes ready, it was time to get the report done, before she forgot all the remarkable symptoms Linda Bates had suffered. *Really? Forget that?* No way could she dismiss that scene and those visions of the writhing woman on the bathroom floor.

Her cell chimed, alerting her once more to the ignored message.

She wondered how the ER visit had gone, and whether the doctor had decided to keep Linda overnight for observation. Suspecting the woman would protest she couldn't go home and stay alone or that she would undoubtedly die in the process, Rachel was relieved she wasn't there to watch the attempted extrication process. Perhaps, they would call dear Bill to come fetch her.

She glanced at her cell again and called her voice mail. A familiar-sounding voice came forth.

What? Of all people...

Carson Graham, a man she counted only as an acquaintance, at best. How long had it been since they'd spoken? Maybe a couple of months. That's right, it was last spring or early summer. He said he'd been thinking of her lately, wondered how she was doing. If she was up to it, he thought they might get together in the near future. Maybe go out for a drink some evening. He hoped she was doing well, and he'd check back with her soon. Goodbye.

Rachel stared at the screen, saved the message and, adding him to her contact list, disconnected from voice mail. How strange...the timing. She hadn't thought of Carson since unexpectedly running into him at the grocery store. A nice man, and admittedly, a rather attractive one at that.

Distracted then and unable to focus on the patient report, she spun around in her desk chair and stared into near space. How long had it been since his wife died? Something like five years...yes, it had been about that long.

Rachel recalled when they had first met, during her time teaching nursing students on the oncology floor at the Kansas University Medical Center. There he and his wife seemed to live during her last run of treatment for acute myelogenous leukemia, a terrible disease, particularly in older adults. How difficult it had been for them going through 'salvage therapy' with Leukemzumab, a novel drug which might prolong a patient's life by a few months. It shortened that woman's life for sure. The reaction she had to it and the side effects were just awful. She died abruptly in her husband's arms, shortly after commencing treatment, her leukemia blasting, short of breath, and delirious.

Rachel had stayed with them that evening, after her nursing students departed, providing what comfort care she could to the dying woman. And to her husband. She recalled vowing then she would never allow herself to go through that, nor would she encourage such treatment for a loved one. At least, not until the drug companies could demonstrate improvements in such medications' side effects.

So grateful for her compassionate care, Carson had asked if he could stay in touch, if she would mind or think it was appropriate. She didn't mind, at the time, and no it wasn't considered inappropriate. Usually, they discussed how he was doing, his feelings, his wife's disease, and the treatments they'd undertaken. But he hadn't called frequently, not after about the sixth-month anniversary of her death. Otherwise, their paths had crossed only occasionally in the suburbs where they both lived.

Then came her divorce. Somehow Carson found out about the whole saga, and the calls picked up. Exhausted at the time and fearing her lawyer husband would make an issue of Carson's interest, she shied away from anything remotely construed as a romantic entanglement. How her husband kept track of her comings and goings, while usually soused, she could never figure out. But, apparently he had. The thought of an investigator tailing her around had always been unsettling. And yet, she couldn't swear that had actually happened. Thank God those tumultuous days were over. Three years ago, but it seemed like another lifetime. Someone else's life.

So, now here he was again—nice, considerate, and yes, good-looking Carson.

But not tonight. She would wait to return his call or wait for him to call again. Then she'd decide. Tonight was hers alone. After she finished her wine, and entered her home visit data, of course.

Another flash of lightning…then a remote roll of thunder. The storm was nearing its end.

Four

Sunday

Scanning through emails, she landed on one which caught her eye: 'Neighborhood Alert: Internet interruption'. What was this all about? The message had come in around midnight, several hours after she'd fallen in bed. Rachel quickly grasped that, due to the previous evening's storm, their area had experienced an interruption of internet service which had been restored around four a.m. Good thing, but many hours of interruption was rather unusual. She'd completed her patient's online form the evening before and hit send. Had it gone through then?

She got up and returned to her kitchen for a fresh cup of coffee. She needed another jolt that morning. Having slept hard, dead to the world, she never heard the second round of thunderstorms roll through shortly after midnight. Awakening later than usual that morning, she'd gone out for a brisk walk and returned to check emails and finish desk work before lunch. She now wondered if her completed report had actually gotten sent. Cradling hot, fresh coffee, she ambled back to her office.

Settling in, she pulled up Advanced Education's website, tapped in her pin, and her account information popped up. A list of patients formed the left column, each person's name a hyperlink.

She clicked on Linda's name and watched the page transform to a landscape-oriented report, completed, and to the right the Adverse Events column, reactions or side effects patients might experience which must be reported to the company. There she confirmed all the complaints Linda had expressed, which were considerable. Rachel noted her objective assessments—Linda's appearance, her vital signs, lack of swelling or rash, ability to move all extremities, etcetera. In her opinion, a well-done report. And it had been sent, either last evening or eventually during the night as she slept, when her internet was finally restored.

Without giving it much thought, Rachel hit the print button and ran off Linda's report, all four pages due to her reactions, and filed it with her others. Taking a moment to thumb through her files, she estimated she had at least several hundred or so printed reports and made a mental note to visit the office supply store that week for more paper and file folders.

It was surprising that, in a short year and a half of teaching she'd accumulated that many patients. But she'd been busy, often called to teach small groups in doctors' offices, or office nurses who might assist patients with their medication, or individual patients in their homes. Several of her clients called regularly, requiring reassurance about the drug's effectiveness, questions regarding self-injection, or those who just needed to talk. Those she didn't mind; that was the setup, was part of her role.

But she also got calls at all hours from patients complaining of side effects, which she addressed, but who were also gently instructed to call Dr. Reynolds' office the next day. Usually that worked, but on occasion her instructions weren't met with kind words, in return. That was hard, especially in the middle of the night. Going back to sleep after such a call often strained several hours.

In recent months, she'd also been asked by a drug rep to help staff the company's booth, promoting the osteoporosis medication at several local or regional medical meetings. There was pressure on the rep to get the word out on the medication's newer indication, remind professionals it wasn't just for inflammatory-variant osteoarthritis. It was fun, on occasion, though she wasn't paid for her time tending the booth. Still, she met doctors and nurses who frequented such meetings, which opened doors to more patients. All of that kept her just about as busy as she preferred to be at this time.

Glancing at her wall clock, Rachel realized she'd spent more time than she intended on that task. She exited the website, saving her work before closing out.

She would call the company tomorrow and make sure everything went through as it appeared it had. But today she'd touch base with the kids, no doubt sleeping off their respective Saturday nights. She'd give them until that evening to recover and become conversant with their mother.

Now, it was time to make some lunch and get ready to watch her favorite NFL team. What a season it might be!

FIVE

Monday

The canned music played as Rachel sat on hold. She had determined it would be best to call them first, inform them of what had happened Saturday afternoon in case Linda called about her symptoms and intolerance of the medication. Dr. Reynolds' nurse picked up.

"This is Carol, Dr. Reynolds' nurse."

"Hi Carol, Rachel Quinn here."

"Oh, hi Rachel. You're calling about one of our OP patients?"

"That's right, Linda Bates. I went out Saturday to teach her about taking her OAinvar. Things didn't go so well, in fact it was rather wild, and I thought I'd let you know in case she calls."

"Okay, then. I'm not surprised. She's called several times over the last month about the whole process of taking the med. So, what happened?"

Resolved to be succinct, Rachel launched into a description of the situation, and how the teaching session progressed, or regressed as the case may be. Quiet on the other end, Carol interrupted only to clarify certain points, then let out a long sigh.

"Sounds like quite a scene. Has she called you since then?"

"No, and frankly I'm relieved she hasn't. I'm not sure whether they kept her in overnight or sent her back home. With her mother in Las Vegas, I was hoping they would contact her husband if she needed company, but I haven't heard."

"Okay. We'll take it from here. I'll let Dr. Reynolds know about this. She may want to call you back."

"Sure. Any time. You have my cell number."

"Thanks, Rachel. Later."

Rachel disconnected. The next call would take care of all she needed to do to follow up the Linda saga, then she could get on with her schedule for the new week, and the six new patients who were lined up for individual teaching, as well as an office session scheduled with five others. She retreated to her kitchen for a coffee refresh.

Having returned to her desk and pulled up Advance Education's website, she again confirmed that her report on Linda Bates was complete and appeared to have been sent. She dialed the main number. She was efficiently transferred to a teaching coordinator who extended a friendly, but professional, greeting and asked if Rachel would hold while she pulled up her records, and the patient she was referring to.

Back on the line, she inquired, "What question do you have?"

Rachel began, "I wrote up the report late Saturday, and due to a storm here and a prolonged internet interruption that evening, I want to make sure you've received it."

"Yes, we have it here."

"The patient Linda Bates experienced quite a few side effects immediately after the injection. That's reflected in the adverse events column there. I know it's long, but I thought it was appropriate to note everything that happened for your records. She demanded I send her to the ER, which I did, even though I didn't think it was necessary. Nor did the paramedics who arrived, who had experience with her frequent calls. But the patient was insistent, so they finally agreed to take her in."

The coordinator remained silent through Rachel's explanation, then asked, "Did you also call in the AEs Saturday evening?"

"Call in?"

"Yes, call the reporting desk. They're here six days a week, from seven A to ten P to take down such information."

Rachel sat speechless on the other end. She'd never called in her reports. What were they asking now? "I've always transmitted my reports through the website, indicating any adverse reactions in the AE column."

The woman's voice held a stern edge. "You're not to put the AEs on the form. You're to call them in."

"Then, why is that column, clearly labeled, on the form?"

Avoiding Rachel's direct question, she said, "The policy is to call in any AEs. I'll have to check on this and call you back."

Before Rachel could counter or question the woman further, the call ended.

She sat staring at the phone. Without delay, she closed out Linda's chart, and opened the two most recent patients she'd instructed. Neither had complained of any side effects after their first injection, so their AE columns bore the notation, 'none'. But she'd hadn't left it blank. There was a woman, however, several months before…maybe in July. She quickly pulled out her calendar, found the date she thought was right, and pulled up that patient's chart. And there it was, a notation in the adverse events column regarding a mild headache. No other side effects. She hadn't called in that encounter, either.

The phone rang again.

Rachel picked up and heard the same woman's voice. No cordial greeting this time.

"Ms. Quinn, there seems to be a problem."

Rachel managed, "Oh," before the woman went on.

"You are supposed to call in all adverse events to the person on duty. They record what happens during a teaching session. We don't use the AE column on the form."

Rachel interrupted, "I understand, but why is that column still on the form? I always record any reactions there. I didn't know I was required to call in, also."

"Oh, yes. That's in your contract."

Her contract? She had looked it over, sure, before signing, but didn't recall any statement requiring her to call in after any or all visits. *Where is that thing anyway?*

"Well, I read my contract before signing, of course, but don't remember seeing anything about calling in."

"You must not have read it very carefully, or perhaps you're forgetful. But it's there, clearly spelled out."

"I beg your pardon. I'm not forgetful. Certainly not about things that happen to patients I'm teaching, or how to perform my job."

"Well, something happened to your understanding."

Furious at the woman's condescending tone, Rachel strained to hold her temper. "I'll be glad to call in my reports of patients' reactions going forward. That's fine with me. I can't change what is already done but will approach it differently from now on."

"I'm not sure about all that. I'll be back in touch." Again, she disconnected before Rachel could answer, or attempt a civil 'goodbye'.

It was time to replenish her coffee, or maybe grab something stronger?

After throwing out the cold coffee, she paced her family room, and wrestled with a sense of foreboding. This situation did not portend well. The coordinator's tone worried her. Would someone else call, reprimand her, admonish her to do a better job? That she could handle, but what if something else happened?

She abruptly stopped pacing, and nearly sprinted to her office and shoved open the closet door. Searching her files for the teaching company folder, she found her contract just as the phone rang again. *Damn.* She wanted to review the contract and have it in front of her, open to the appropriate page, before discussing this further with them.

Clutching the contract, she stepped to her desk and picked up the call.

Her heart pounded. "Yes, this is Rachel Quinn."

"Rachel, this is Joyce McClellan, VP for education. I'm calling back about the situation you encountered this past weekend during a teaching session."

"Yes."

Momentarily, Rachel relaxed, hopeful this woman would be more reasonable, and they could discuss this whole mess like two professionals. Her relief was short lived.

"I'm afraid this poses a significant problem for the company. At this point, we don't know the full extent of what may happen."

"Extent of what may happen?"

Her tone shrill then, the VP continued, "That's right. We may have to pay a large fine for each such occurrence. That is a major problem for all of us." She paused, then said, "Due to this development, we're relieving you of your duties as an instructor, as of now."

Stunned, Rachel dropped into her desk chair, thankful it was handy. "I beg your pardon?"

"We don't require your teaching services any longer." With that the other woman hung up.

Unbelievable. Inside of one hour since she'd initiated the call to them, honest about her reporting, she'd been chastised, her memory had been questioned, and now she sat—fired. Never had she been let go from a professional position. Never. And for doing the right thing?

What exactly had she overlooked in that contract? As she raised the thin document, her hands trembled, but she managed to speed read the first two pages. Routine contract verbiage. She reviewed the section on page three referring to completion of the online form. Then she saw it, in smaller print, and a different font, toward the bottom of page three, indented as though an afterthought: 'The educator will promptly call the teaching company with any adverse events. The phone desk is available from seven a.m. to ten p.m., six days a week, except Sundays.' No mention or admonition to avoid use of the Adverse Event column on their online form. She continued reading through the remainder of the contract and signature page. Not exactly damning, save for her lack of calling.

Why don't they also want the reactions recorded on the proper form? And what is this about a large fine?

Alarmed, Rachel rose, glad she had printed and retained all her patient reports. They might come in handy.

Two hours later, after returning from a vigorous walk, Rachel sat at her desk and pulled up the teaching company website. She tapped in her pin and stared at the screen. Nothing happened. She tried several other entry points, including a recent email. Nothing. She'd been officially blocked. They sure hadn't wasted any time kicking her off.

Neither did she waste further time before pulling all her files from her office closet, bundling them down to her basement safe room, and locking them in a metal file cabinet there.

This whole situation started ugly, and now seemed poised to turn a lot uglier.

Six

Tuesday

The day dragged on—loitering around, antagonizing her, amounting to nothing. The hours crept by, not adequately consumed by two workout periods, nor any amount of tidying up her desk which had begged for attention in recent weeks. Eventually, evening arrived.

Suddenly without work, set adrift—she'd never found herself in such a situation. Always prepared, always organized, she made a practice of securing one position before leaving another. Of course, she had prudently prepared for potential 'disasters' by diligently setting aside funds each month. Though the thought of what just happened had never occurred to her. So, there was a nest egg, but she was loath to consider raiding it. Sure, the divorce had provided an additional 'insurance' fund in case she found herself unemployed, and unwanted. But that trust was not accessible on a moment's notice and was a story for another day. This was a mess. And she hardly knew how to handle herself, how to behave.

Rachel sat in her office and stared at her desktop screen. There was no doubt she'd been cut off from the website, but…she picked up her cell, tapped a similar icon on her phone screen, and up popped the site. *Why hadn't it worked twice before? Never mind. Here it is.* With a sense of urgency, she tapped in her pin and quickly opened her account. Up came her list of patients for the past six months. Tapping again, she accessed her entire patient list without obstruction. Scrolling through the list, she confirmed that each patient's data was complete and preserved. *My, what a surprise! Now, what to do with it?*

Just a few more taps and swipes and she found the list of other instructors, and their cohorts of patients. *Why hadn't the company cut off this access as well? And why did I have access to their records in the first place?* She couldn't determine that now, but it was important that she still could get in. Drilling down she viewed a few of their reports. Low and behold, many of them had also completed the Adverse Events column. She paused, wondering if they, too, were among the ranks of the now unemployed. Perhaps the company had surveyed the situation over the past two days and found the other violators. Wouldn't it be great if she could speak with those other instructors?

Then a single thought intruded. That she could still access the other instructors' files and patient lists most assuredly represented a HIPPA violation on the part of the company. Armed with this information she could inflict considerable damage upon them, including fines and imprisonment, if they threatened to come after her. That thought buoyed her mood a bit, and her pulse. But she needed to refrain from such ideas at the moment and stay focused.

The next thing to do was make sure she secured this and could maintain access going forward. Somehow, she needed to back up this information. This might prove essential if the 'infraction' she'd committed was pursued by the teaching company, or heavens, the drug company itself. Most disturbing was their statement about a large fine…per occurrence. Would they try to turn that to her? God forbid.

Her cell chimed with an incoming call. This time she quickly recognized the number—Carson Graham again. She'd expected maybe several weeks before he would contact her once more, if he did at all. This was definitely intriguing. And right then, she needed a friend.

She picked up. "Hi there."

Apparently surprised, he paused before answering, "Well, hi. I wasn't sure you'd know who was calling. I wondered if you'd gotten my message the other evening."

"Yes, I did. And it surprised me. But Saturday was rather strange, and I just couldn't call back then. I apologize."

"No need for that. I wanted to leave you the message and thought I'd wait to hear back from you. But yesterday you were on my mind, and I thought I'd touch base again and make sure you were okay."

Stunned by the coincidence of his apparent telepathy, Rachel sat speechless.

After a few moments, Carson spoke. "Rachel, are you still there? Are you okay?"

"I'm here, but I don't know if you'd say I'm okay."

"What's happened?"

"It's a long story, and frankly, I've about had it today. I haven't slept well for two nights, and I'm very tired."

"Rachel, what's happened? You don't sound like yourself."

"I'm not sure I am myself right now. It's about my position with a company—former company—where I did patient teaching."

"Did?"

"That's right. I've been relieved of my duties. Fired."

"That's hard to believe. What went wrong?"

"How much time do you have?" Rachel quipped without thinking.

"All the time you need."

Suddenly realizing Carson's calls likely signaled more than just checking in on an acquaintance, she hesitated. Should she tell him this whole ridiculous story? As she hemmed and hawed, feelings of being utterly alone surfaced and without hesitating further, she launched into an edited version of the saga.

He listened patiently and about five or so minutes later asked how she felt about the whole ordeal. Not peppering her with questions, nor grilling her about details, he waited for her to confide her feelings. This was a new experience. She couldn't recall a man ever expressing such sincere concern about her feelings. Certainly not her former husband, who spent most of his time talking about his lawyering dilemmas. Or he was drunk and didn't care how anyone else felt.

After pausing, she said, "Frankly, it feels crappy."

His soft chuckle helped.

"It feels like the rug's been yanked out from under me. After making this beyond-the-call-of-duty effort to teach this patient, and documenting all that transpired, it feels like a gut punch. And now

I realize I hadn't studied the contract as closely as I should have. That was my omission, I admit. How stupid of me."

"Rachel, you're being too hard on yourself. The contract thing could be a simple oversight. Contract language is convoluted, and most people scan the complicated paragraphs, grasping the gist of the document. Combing over a contract is usually enough to put you to sleep. That's not a big omission on your part. But actually there may be something else going on here."

"Something else?"

"Yeah. You said the woman didn't answer your question about why they retained the side effects column on the form if they weren't using it. That strikes me as strange. Or, at least questionable. That they don't keep their forms up to date. And the deal about having to call in reactions to a phone jockey and not put them on the record. That's also rather suspect. And, of course, the whole sizable fine thing. Something doesn't ring true about this situation."

"I agree. In fact, I've been uneasy since the phone calls yesterday. Still sorting it all out. Maybe I didn't want to admit I might have uncovered something more troubling."

"So, she didn't say what the fine was for, or to which group or organization it would be paid?"

"No, and the last woman who called sounded wigged out, very shrill, but didn't explain anything specific about the threat of a fine."

"And you've been shut out of the website?"

"Yes, completely. But, I have always printed my records, so those are secured. But interestingly, I can still access my patient information, and other teachers' as well, through an app on my cell."

"Have you transferred that yet to any other format or saved it to the cloud?"

"Not yet."

"Maybe I can help with that." He paused, then went on, "What would you say to getting together tomorrow evening for a drink? You can fill me in on more of the details then, and I might suggest some technical strategies which may help."

That whole prospect sounded suddenly very appealing. And reassuring. After a brief pause, Rachel agreed to meet Carson.

They set a time and place, ending their call.

Exhausted, she decided to retire early. Closing out her computer, and killing her office lights, she moved down the hall toward her bedroom. Perhaps tonight she would finally get some solid sleep. The day had just ended on a more positive note than it began. Due to a single, unexpected phone call.

Had she just agreed to a real date?

Seven

Wednesday

The bar and grill gave off a subdued vibe. Dark wood trim, stone accents, leather seating, all geared toward retaining patrons for additional rounds. A fire crackled in a corner fireplace and with the chilly fall evening, Rachel welcomed the warm atmosphere.

She scanned the room for Carson. Arriving purposely ten minutes late, she figured he would already be seated, perhaps drink in hand. The place was modestly busy for a Wednesday evening. She spotted him in an out-of-the-way small booth. Glancing toward the entrance, he saw her, smiled, and rose from his seat. She wound her way through the tables and greeted him with a warm handshake. No hugs permitted, yet.

Settling in, she noted he'd chosen a sport coat and casual knit shirt. Slacks—not jeans—and expensive loafers. He looked as if he'd taken time to prepare for this meeting, not merely throwing on the handiest jacket and landing there. Admittedly, she'd also taken time with her clothing choices, not wishing to appear as if she considered this a bona fide date. But, neither did she want to look as bedraggled as she felt. She finally settled on casual slacks, a seasonal knit top, and a jacket she'd snagged on sale several years before. Relaxed, but not revealing. It was obvious to her they were both concerned with how they signaled the opposite party. Silly, really, as she thought about it. Two middle-aged adults trying to impress, but not acting like they were at all concerned with impressing. *It never changes, does it?* She smiled.

He returned her smile. "You look great."

"Thank you."

"What would you like to have?"

She glanced at the whiskey he nursed. "Oh, let's see what they're offering." Quickly surveying the wine and spirits list, she chose a familiar Chardonnay. He signaled their waiter, who took her order with dispatch. Those preliminaries over, they gave each other appraising looks.

He started. "So, it's been a while."

"Yes, it has."

"You've been well?"

"I'd say yes, considering."

He didn't probe further regarding all her statement could imply. "How did today go? Any more news from the front?"

"No. However, I did sleep better last night. Thanks to our brief conversation, I'm sure."

That seemed to please him. His face softened. "Any more thoughts about what I said?"

"You mean that there may be something else going on, or how you might help with record transfer or preservation?"

"Both, actually."

"Well, sure, I've been mulling over your comments, and had some ideas myself about their motivations. Are you going to share your thoughts further?"

"If you're interested."

"I am." The waiter returned with her wine, inquired about any other needs, and retreated.

Carson began. "It struck me that, if they wanted to know of reactions patients had to the medication, they would want you to record those, so they'd have accurate documentation. Which they would need to transmit to the drug company, or which the drug company could access also for their records, right?"

"Yes, that's what you'd expect."

"So, if they don't want reactions notated there, why not? And, if the instructors are only to call the symptoms or reactions in to a phone desk, how certain is it that the person manning the phone will accurately record your data?"

"Exactly."

"To clarify, they told you the phone receptionist is the one who would record the data you were to call in, correct?"

"That's what the one woman said."

"Okay, so it's not much of a leap to think that they want to screen the instructors' calls, and probably record only the data they want to transmit to the drug company, which, of course, has to report adverse reactions to the FDA."

"Of course, I see where you're going. And, further," Rachel posed, "what if they're in cahoots? What if the drug company instructed them to compile data and report it in just such a manner to them? Then they could submit only favorable data, sprinkled with minimal expected side effects, to the FDA, which is monitoring post-market patient usage and tolerance. No undesirable online or paper trail—"

Carson interrupted, "Right. An increased number of adverse reactions could kill a new drug, or get it pulled from the market, I would suspect, if the reactions are judged to be too frequent or severe."

"Absolutely."

"Another consideration. Do you know whether the medication was pushed through the FDA approval process quickly or without much scrutiny?"

"No, I don't know that. I'm fairly well-acquainted with our area drug rep, however, who visits various medical offices regularly. She might know. I can, at least, ask her."

"Since you've been removed, will you have much contact with her?"

"Oh, I can position myself conveniently so I do. At least once. I worked closely with Dr. Reynolds, the orthopedist who runs an osteoporosis clinic. I'm friends with her and several of her staff. If I appear in her office soon, she won't know whether I'm still employed by the teaching company or not. I can lay in wait for the rep."

Carson grinned. "You sound like you relish the prospect."

"I guess I do. Zera's friendly, but well, a bit narcissistic. She'll find out soon enough that I'm no longer with the education company, but perhaps she'll talk before the veil comes down."

"Worth a try." Carson asked, "Zera? That's unusual. Her real name?"

"I have no idea, actually. You imply she's adopted a stage name?"

Carson shrugged.

"At any rate, I'm up for giving it a whirl."

Rachel sipped her wine and shifted gears. "So, tell me what you're doing now. You haven't mentioned your work. Still at it?" Admittedly, it was always dangerous to wade into such a subject when you've likely forgotten the essential details, which she had.

"Yes, and no. You obviously recall I started the tech security company fifteen years ago."

Oh, right, computers and security. Fragments of conversations from five years ago drifted back. Hopefully, she didn't project too confused an expression.

Apparently not noticing, he went on, "I sold the company's three branches earlier this year to several of my younger partners. I was fortunate to have gotten in on the ground level when I did. It's gone very well, is on solid footing, and they're eager to take growth in new directions. Part of the deal is that I stay on as a senior advisor and consultant, so it seems to be the best of both worlds. My schedule is lighter, and I can pursue other interests."

He leveled a look at Rachel. She grew warm under his gaze.

"Tech security, how coincidental. So what suggestions, then, do you have regarding securing my files in different form? And maybe the app on my phone? You mentioned that last night."

"I did. Given what I've seen in the industry, I would strongly recommend we back up your files in several forms. To the cloud, for one. Download them, if possible, onto a jump drive, maybe several, and secure them at another location. The basics, you know. Do you have a safe deposit box?"

"Yes, I do."

"Good, then you can have access rather easily. We can look at several other strategies, too."

"Okay. So, what do your services usually run?"

Carson smiled. "I think we can work out something reasonable in your case."

Not sure where this was going, but intrigued, Rachel smiled. "Okay, but I don't want to consume a lot of your time."

"I have the time, no problem there."

"You know, I had another thought. It might be a good idea to check the FDA site, either under the pharmaceutical company's name or the drug's name to see what reporting, if any, has been filed so far. Could be interesting."

"That sounds like a good place to start…after we secure your files." He took a swig of his bourbon and got right to the point. "What would you say if I come over tomorrow evening for a while and we get started? Then you don't have to drag all your paperwork to my office. And you can show me your contract as well. If you care to, that is."

"I think that's a great idea. I'd appreciate that. Certainly, more convenient for me. How about seven, then?"

"Works for me." He took another sip and smiled, "Another glass of wine for you?"

Fasten your seatbelt, an annoying little voice advised.

E<small>IGHT</small>

Thursday

Not sure quite what to expect, Rachel fussed over her bar set up. She had arranged her whiskey selections just so, but avoided a prominent display of unnecessary quantity. Not wanting to suggest an evening of boozing as her plan, she'd put away several other liquor bottles from the large antique credenza—her dry bar, which created a transition between her kitchen and the adjoining family room. But she left out several lead crystal decanters for effect. Satisfied with the appearance, she stepped away. And, of course, she had tidied up otherwise after her immensely busy day being unemployed—day three, but who's counting?

This time she opted to dress as if she wasn't making too much of his visit. Jeans, and a casual tunic top, in a color which complemented her green eyes, of course. Otherwise, she made no further efforts.

Who am I kidding? she wondered. Perhaps, though, she hadn't lost her sense of self-appraisal or humor…yet. Or so she'd like to think.

The doorbell chimed. She counted to ten before walking to the front hall to answer. Pulling open the heavy door, she beheld Carson standing there, keeping an appropriate distance from the door. But not looking too like a door-to-door salesman lurking ten feet back on the walk.

"Come in." He didn't hesitate.

Once inside, Rachel led him to her kitchen and watched as he surveyed her space in a sweeping glance.

Turning to her, he said, "This is nice. The tall ceilings, impressive stone fireplace. I like it. Have you lived here long?"

"It's been about two years. And thank you. There's enough room for me and an occasional visitor, three bedrooms, one up."

"I've noticed the neighborhood when driving by but haven't ever been inside the gates." He smiled.

"Yeah, it has atmosphere for sure. And security. Great neighbors, too. Almost exclusively adults, single professionals, empty nesters, you know."

"So, your kids are out of the house, now?"

"Yes. My daughter Amanda's just started at Grinnell in Iowa, but I suspect she'll come home regularly at first—"

"Maybe not," he inserted.

She smiled and shrugged. "Josh, the eldest, moved out officially when he started law school last fall."

He nodded understanding, then said, "I'm still in the house. Guess I'm rationalizing that the boys want me to keep it. Suppose I haven't wanted to go through everything yet, even though it's been five years now. When you keep busy, you think you can't find the time. Of course now, I really don't have any excuses."

He turned back to Rachel and gave her a look.

"Oh, you'll know when you're ready to dive in. It'll come." She paused, then asked, "Care for something to drink?"

"Just ice water, thanks. Maybe something else later?"

"Sure." *Later? When does he think we'll wind this up?* He obviously came feeling flexible or wanted her to get into a flexible mood.

As she prepared two ice waters, she asked, "So, your sons, are they out of college?"

"Yeah, Greg's in accounting. Has been with a firm for two years since graduating. Geoff is getting there. He's a senior at KU, premed. Taking the MCAT soon, going through the whole application process."

"That's great. So, you may be supporting a medical student for a while."

"There's that risk."

"I'm sure you're very proud of them. Is Greg here in Kansas City?"

"Yeah."

"Married?"

"No, not yet."

Beverages prepared, and the family assessments done, she suggested, "Shall we go into the office? I'll show you the records. I assume you want to go ahead and get started."

"Lead the way." He followed her down the hall and into her very organized office. Of course, she had put away all other sensitive material in anticipation of his visit. And she'd retrieved the print copies of all her patient records, names covered, from her basement safe room. Everything pertinent was at hand.

Glancing around the well-appointed room, he observed, "Very nice. I like your desk and bookshelves. They have presence." *Presence? He means they're big and give off a masculine vibe...true.* More like 'presents', though, from her ex—washout from the divorce settlement. He added, "You keep a neat space."

"Not usually. But I have plenty of time now to straighten up." That elicited a soft chuckle from Carson. Indicating a rather tall stack of papers on a narrow antique sideboard, she said, "Here are the printed reports...I've selected several to show you. And there are two new jump drives we can use and, of course, my contract."

He picked up the contract first and glanced through the four-page document. His brow knitted when he reached page three, his eyes studying the lower part of the sheet. "Hum," he said, glancing at the signature page and handing it back to her.

Rachel took the document and a seat in a nearby club chair.

Still standing in the middle of the room, Carson said, "Looks exactly like you said the other night. That paragraph about calling in to the phone desk is there, but certainly minimized in position, different font character and size. Almost looks like an afterthought, or something they didn't want emphasized. Or maybe it was inserted later." He paused, then went on, "Perhaps even after you agreed to work for them, or after you signed the contract. They could have sent you this copy after you signed, just attaching your signature page to the back. Did you keep a copy of your original?"

"Honestly, I can't remember the order in which the paperwork was exchanged. Or, if I duplicated the copy I signed before sending it back. That was not quite two years ago, about a year or so into my divorce action. At times, I was overwhelmed, and frankly, wasn't as fastidious about other details as I would have normally been. But I shouldn't make excuses. I may have it here somewhere but haven't been able to put my hands on it, yet."

She continued, "On Monday, when the woman I spoke to mentioned the 'calling-in requirement', I doubted ever seeing it in my contract. The one I signed. But then I questioned myself, and when I retrieved this contract from my file, I thought it was the original. Now that you mention it, I agree, it may not be."

"That's one possibility. The other, of course, is that the structure of the paragraph doesn't encourage close examination. It's easy to look over and keep going. In which case that was your responsibility, as you said." He looked at Rachel and added, "I can have a forensic document person look it over and see if there are signs it was inserted later."

She stared at him. *Forensic document person?* "That sounds interesting. Here, I'll make a copy and you can take the original. Anything that can help clarify the situation and my vulnerability." She rose from her seat and fed the contract through her printer.

That completed, she suggested, "Why don't I pull up the website so you can see it, even though I'm blocked?"

At her desk then, she typed in the website address and turned to Carson. "Here we are."

He moved to a position directly behind her and leaned forward a bit. Close enough for her to appreciate the faint hint of his aftershave, quite a pleasant scent at that. Refocusing, she added, "So, here on the sign-in page I'll insert my pin, and there you go…'access denied'."

"Right. Have you tried any other routes in?"

"Yes, and none do anything."

"Okay." He stepped back.

Rachel swiveled in her chair and retrieved one report from the top of the short stack on her desk, Linda Bates' document. "Here's an example of how a report looks. You can see the identifying information at the top, including my name there. The columns on each page include the one for adverse events on the far right, and you can clearly see my notations from last Saturday's encounter." Reaching to the stack again, she picked up another from the neat pile. "Here's one…a patient who had a mild headache right after the first injection. I made notation of that also in the AE column." She handed him the documents which he surveyed quickly.

"I see that. So now what we need to do is scan all these reports to one of your jump drives, then duplicate that drive so you can store it off site. How many pages are there here?"

"Actually, four hundred thirty-five reports. More than I thought I had, with average one to three pages per report."

"So, scanning seven hundred fifty to maybe thirteen hundred pages will take some time. Do you have enough paper here to do that while we move on?"

"Yes. I made a run yesterday to buy more."

"Okay, let's get that started." He picked up the stack of papers and moved toward her scanner to begin preparing the documents. "I assume these are in chronological order."

"Yes." She rose to assist him and make sure none were out of whack, and added back the few reports from her desk. That set, and the jump drive plugged in, they began the process.

As the copier whirred along, scanning efficiently, she returned to her desk and pulled up the FDA.gov site. He joined her there, again leaning in over her shoulder to get a better look at the screen.

That aftershave he's wearing…

He asked, "So, what's your best bet about where to start? Think it'll be under the drug company's name…will they give a list of their drugs, or will it just be listed by itself?"

Recovered then, she said "Let's see." After tapping around, and drilling down, she came to the page for Mynard-Drexel Pharmaceuticals. Founded by two retired physicians about ten years ago, it went by M-D Pharma. They had managed to develop three medications since their inception, all three of which remained on the market, and which had enjoyed moderate success. Fairly impressive, actually, that they were able to develop and push through three drugs in just ten years. Certainly, no Zocor or lisinopril, but showing respectable, steadily increasing sales. Upon closer scrutiny, though, it was clear no adverse reports were included there for their three medications.

"Okay, let's try this." She backed out of the company's list and returned to the home page. Typing in the drug name in the search box, they waited as the cumbersome government site processed. Finally, up popped the name 'Arthremimab' at the top of the page. Three short paragraphs below gave standard introductory information, including the trade name, 'OAinvar'.

Date of release to the market—2015. Initial approval was for the inflammatory variant of osteoarthritis, hence the trade name. Since that time, it had also proved beneficial for bone density, noted on many arthritis patients' bone density studies—while controlling for other variables—and gained approval for osteoporosis treatment. That approval had been rather speedy, since it was already on the market and enjoying increasing success treating its original indication, osteoarthritis–inflammatory variant.

Rachel clicked on the 'side effects/adverse reactions' profile. A brief statement appeared, instructing any interested parties to request a form regarding adverse reactions from the FDA. Once that form was completed and submitted online, the inquirer would receive a response usually within ten to fourteen days, excluding weekends and holidays, with the information they had requested, or a statement indicating otherwise.

Rachel and Carson exchanged a look. He stepped back.

"So, there you have it. I'm surprised with all the information about medications available on the internet, the FDA doesn't publish reports of adverse reactions on their site," he said.

"Yeah. Now, I'm really curious. Before I close this out, I'm going to request the form and see what happens. If I receive it, I'll see how convoluted it is, how much personal information I must submit, and maybe then complete it." She turned back to the computer screen, and quickly filled in the blanks requesting the form. Not too bad for a government site. She hit submit, then backed out again to the home page. "Want to see anything else?"

"Nope."

She closed the site. "That was interesting."

"Rather as expected, I'd say."

"Rather." Pushing up from her chair, she asked, "Need a refill on your water, or something stronger?"

"If you have stronger, I'd enjoy that. All this searching government sites has made me anxious."

Smiling, she said, "Follow me."

Once in the kitchen, she indicated the dry bar, "Please, make your selection and I'll get the glasses."

He stood browsing her collection, then picked out a bourbon she usually kept for special occasions. "This one okay?"

"Sure." *Sure, you have expensive tastes.*

Having produced two glasses, she said, "And pour me one, too, please. About a finger, neat."

"Of course." He proceeded to fix their drinks after requesting one ice cube for his. Rachel had taken a seat at her countertop awaiting her drink. He joined her there, scooting his chair closer.

"You said you had information on your cell phone they hadn't blocked yet. Still true?"

"Yeah, at least earlier today. I'll show you…but don't report me for a HIPPA violation."

She rose from her seat and retrieved her cell from the adjacent counter. Returning, she pulled up the app, and after tapping in her pin—different than the one she had to use on the website—her info popped up. Quickly checking another instructor's information, she confirmed it was there, then backed out to her section. He didn't need to see all that other. She turned the screen to him.

"So, how come you're not blocked from that access?"

"I don't have the foggiest idea. It's an app for instructors. We had to download it initially so we'd have access to our records, I guess, from anywhere. Maybe it's not connected to the main website. Or maybe it is just an oversight on their part."

"Hum…mind if I see that?"

"Of course not, but please ignore the individual names."

"I'm sure I won't be able to recite a single name, once I'm off your phone. I don't have that kind of memory."

She doubted that, and watched as he scanned down the pages, swiping the screen every few seconds.

"That's quite a list. It's complete?" he asked, handing the phone back to her.

"Yes, I made sure the other day. Do you think there's a way we can transfer this data to another device or download it to another platform?"

"We won't know for sure without trying. If it's encrypted, we may not be able to. I'll need to work with it to see."

"Now, or later?" she asked, sipping her whiskey.

"Let me see," he said, taking a swig. He commenced swiping again, his brow knitted, apparently totally focused. Rachel watched as he worked, enjoying the whiskey's warmth, the companionship, and Carson's interest in helping her. A bad situation turned good…well, a little good, maybe.

He looked up and extended the phone back to her. "Looks like it may take a bit more work. There's a young man at the company who's excellent with cell technology. Far better than me. I'll have him take a look at it, if you don't mind."

"I'd like to keep hold of it, not that I don't trust you, you understand. This whole app represents a potential HIPPA violation. The access to other instructors' records, and the obvious identifying information on the patients loaded there. I really should have deleted it, and certainly I shouldn't let anyone else have access to it. Technically, that is."

"Of course, I understand completely." He sipped again, which allowed her time to consider her options, then suggested, "If you're comfortable with the idea, you could come by my office in the next couple of days, and while you're there, he could check it out under your watchful eye." He paused, then added, "If you want to know how to transfer it elsewhere, you're going to have to let someone in tech security take a look at it, maybe fiddle with it a bit, then tell you if it's retainable, other than on your cell."

"That sounds good. I don't think I should wait very long, though. They might discover their oversight and block me out any day now."

"True, they might." Carson had slung his left arm over the back of Rachel's chair as they'd chatted about her cell phone, though she'd hardly noticed.

"How about tomorrow?" he suggested. "Otherwise, we're into next week."

"Tomorrow sounds good." She moved from her chair at the counter and rinsed her glass in the sink. There would be no second rounds that evening. "Let's go check on the scanning progress, shall we?"

"Why not?" Putting his empty glass on the counter, he followed her to her office.

NINE

Friday

Traffic was unusually heavy that morning for nearly ten o'clock. Rachel maneuvered her Accord through the route to Carson's office, circumventing several construction zones, realizing she'd arrive there fifteen minutes later than he expected her. Couldn't be helped.

She'd placed a call to the drug rep Zera before departing home. Not unexpectedly, it had gone straight to voicemail, but hopefully she would respond soon. It might prove informative before discussing this again with Carson and his young techie guy. Exiting the interstate, she spotted the street leading to the cluster of office buildings housing Carson's company headquarters. She made her way up the sloping drive and confirmed the address over the entrance. Within a few minutes she was inside, taking the elevator to the eighth or top floor, the entirety of which his company occupied. *Does he perhaps own the whole building?*

She approached the reception desk and spoke with a comely young female manning the fort. "Mr. Graham, please. Rachel Quinn. I have an appointment."

"Yes, Ms. Quinn, would you take a seat and I'll page him."

As she made herself comfortable and adjusted her shoulder bag, her cell chimed. Drug rep Zera Riordan. Rather than shunting it to voice mail, she picked up. Carson materialized at the corner of the reception desk just as she answered. She gave him a slight nod.

He stood close, observing her reactions.

"Yes, hello, Zera. Thanks for calling back."

"Of course. What can I do?"

"I have several questions for you, but I'm at an appointment now. May we speak later this morning, or sometime this afternoon?"

"Sure. Questions about what?"

"Oh, a couple of things on OAinvar."

"Problems with your patients getting theirs?"

"No, another issue." Out of the corner of her eye, she noted a small smile crease Carson's face.

"Well, okay, sure. How about after two? I'm doing a lunch today, but then I'll be free. Just dropping off some sample packs at a couple of places after that. I'll give you a call."

"Is one of your stops Reynolds' office?"

"Matter of fact, it is. They've run out of samples. So, why don't I call you after that?"

"Good. Thanks." They disconnected.

Not just good—great! There was enough time to finish here, get there, and lay in wait. Rachel gathered her bag and stood.

Carson gestured down the hall without speaking. He escorted her, inquiring as they went about her morning, but only in the most general terms. Passing multiple private offices, she noted a few younger associates busy that Friday. Other offices sat empty, their occupants on assignment or engaged elsewhere?

Once they reached his corner, he stepped aside as she entered. At a glance, she took in the generous office space. She stopped, not presuming to sit before he offered. Besides, she noticed there was an obvious decision to make—occupy one of two chairs in front of his desk, or make her way to a small loveseat and club chairs positioned near a fireplace at the opposite end of the room.

One and a half walls were framed in large glass panels providing Carson and his subordinates or clients a spectacular view of south Kansas City, Missouri and nearby Johnson County, Kansas. A perfect position from which to attend to many well-situated clients who likely had all kinds of computer and technology security issues. He had obviously done well, had prospered. She felt his eyes on her. Rachel turned and faced him directly.

"What a lovely view."

"Yes. It can get a bit bright with the west sun blazing in, especially in the summer, but these help." He stepped to the window, pressed a button, and electronic shades lowered, muting the light but not obscuring the view. The perfect solution.

She smiled. "You have all the bases covered."

He reset the shades, which rose again—it was early enough in the day to eliminate worries about the hot September sun—and moved toward her.

"Care to sit here?" He motioned to the loveseat.

Rachel made a calculated move to the middle of the small sofa and placed her bag next to her on the upholstered piece. Carson took one of the leather club chairs.

"So, I presume that was the drug rep Zera you referred to the other day?"

"Yes. I called her earlier and, of course, she called back just as I arrived. As you no doubt heard, she'll call again this afternoon to address my questions."

"Probably wise to keep it general."

Her lips parted but, in the moment, restraint reined her in. *Should I tell him about my planned ambush?*

He gave her a quizzical look. "You were going to say?"

"Oh, I agree. I thought I'd focus on the approval process. Of course, she may already know about my being fired from the teaching company. Word in the drug rep world travels very fast."

"Are you going to tell her about your conversations with the company from earlier in the week?"

"Probably not. Unless she brings it up."

"That may be best." He smiled, then added, "Brandon will be in shortly. I only told him you had an app on your phone related to your work that we'd like him to look at. Tell us if it can be transferred to a different platform or format."

As he finished, there was a soft knock at the door. Carson rose and strode across the room. There stood a tall, slender young man, who couldn't be any older than Rachel's son Josh. He seemed shy, facing the founder of the company. Carson welcomed him into the office.

As he entered, he spied Rachel perched on the loveseat and stopped. Carson gestured for him to proceed to join them there.

Rachel stood and offered her hand.

"Hi, I'm Rachel Quinn."

"Brandon Knight, Ms. Quinn."

"Well, now that we're introduced, let's sit and go over what exactly Ms. Quinn needs of us," Carson said.

Brandon only nodded.

Carson took the lead, and continued, "Ms. Quinn is a nurse educator. She has an app on her cell phone related to her work. It contains considerable sensitive information on a number of patients whom she has instructed. It's best if she removes it from her phone and transfers it to a more protected platform or site. After you look at the app, we'd like your opinion on that. But she can't relinquish her phone to us. The assessment needs to be done in front of her."

Brandon focused on Carson as he explained all that and paused before answering. Finally, he spoke. "Sure, I can take a look. It'll probably be about fifteen minutes to give you an answer. But sometimes we can't complete our assessment without transferring the information to another device."

Rachel inserted, "I'd rather you not do that today. If you determine that's necessary, then I'll need to schedule for another time. The information is HIPPA-protected."

"That's cool," Brandon affirmed.

"Are we in agreement, then, to go ahead?" Carson asked.

"Yes." She handed Carson her phone.

Carson showed Brandon to a small conference table set off to one side nearer the window expanse, left him with the phone, and rejoined Rachel. "Would you like coffee while we wait?"

"Sure, that sounds good."

"Brandon?"

"A Diet Pepsi, sir. Thanks."

Carson departed for his desk, and after relaying their request over the phone intercom, returned to the conversation area.

Exactly fifteen minutes later, Brandon stood from his chair and rejoined them. He handed Rachel her phone and pronounced, "It's a complicated app, but I think we can deal with it. It's encrypted, but there are ways around that. Do you know of any legal issues with moving it?"

Suspecting there would be, Rachel said, "Perhaps," then

turned to Carson, "What do you think?"

He weighed in. "You raise a good point, Brandon. We likely will need an opinion regarding that, but Ms. Quinn and I will discuss it and contact you again if we want to proceed."

Brandon's cue to depart. He nodded, retrieved his Pepsi and moved toward the door. "Thanks, Mr. Graham. Just let me know." He disappeared through the door, easing it shut behind him.

Carson turned to Rachel. "I thought as much but didn't want to pull our legal team in before we got Brandon' opinion. Frankly, from our first conversation, I thought you might be heading in that direction. But I wanted to look at your records and make sure you were comfortable proceeding. Sometimes when you poke around, you make matters worse." He paused. When she didn't respond, he added, "You can stop now, let things lie, and see what happens. That's a legitimate position to take."

Considering Carson's comments, Rachel mulled her options.

"I don't think I can just let go of this now and ignore what may be going on. I'm still waiting for the FDA form about adverse reactions reporting. That may give me some insight into whether their numbers jive with the instructors' data submissions. So, I need to retain the other instructors' information to help determine if the drug company numbers are too low for expected side-effects or reactions. Then there's the whole issue of a too-speedy approval process. Basically, I'd just like to secure the records before I decide how much further I'm willing to probe."

"Sounds as if you'd like to proceed. Why don't you give it some thought over the weekend, and then let me know your decision?"

"I agree. Sleeping on it for a couple of nights may change my thinking. One thing, though, Carson…please don't feel obligated to stay in this situation. Certainly, if I go forward, I'll need your company's services, but I don't want to cause you any legal difficulties. Such as pulling you into a possible HIPPA-violation case. Right now, my ability to access the phone app likely constitutes a violation on their part. If I move that to another platform or device, or even if I retain the current app, then I become just as guilty as them. It could get very messy, and expensive."

"Precisely. In which case, you would be best armed with our

legal department's advice and preparation. They know how to navigate such waters. And you're not pulling me into anything," he finished with a broad smile.

Reassured, but a bit overwhelmed by the breadth of the problem, Rachel returned his smile and stood.

"I hope you're ready, quite possibly, for a rough ride."

Escorting her to the door, he said, "I could use a little excitement right now."

Ten

Her thoughts spinning, Rachel hardly noticed anything as she drove. The familiarity of her route provided much needed thinking time. After grabbing a quick sandwich at a handy Panera's, she embarked on her journey across several suburbs to the target location. Her gut told her to pursue this effort, her brain told her to exercise caution. Maybe a phone call would work just as well.

~ ~ ~ ~

Having been admitted by the receptionist with a friendly wave, Rachel rounded the corner and greeted Dr. Reynolds' nurse Carol.

"Hi there. How's your day?"

"Not bad at all for a Friday," Carol said. "Yours?"

"Good, good. Any big plans for the weekend?"

Carol frowned. "Cleaning out my garage. Yuck."

"But you'll feel so good when it's done."

"Right. I'll focus on that. Had any lunch yet?"

"Yeah, I'm good."

Carol checked her desk calendar. "You have patients coming in today? I don't have any down."

"No, no, I'm here to wait for Zera Riordan. She said she'd be by with some samples. Have a few questions for her. Nothing much."

Carol nodded. "Well, relax and help yourself to the leftover cookies in the kitchen if you want. Reynolds isn't here this afternoon. She's on call this weekend and is already over at the hospital on a case."

"Sounds good, thanks."

Rachel made her way through the office hall and took up position in the kitchen, with a good view of the sample closet. And the medication fridge where Zera would have to place the injectable med. She glanced at her watch. *Perfect timing.* It was one forty-five and no doubt she'd hear the bubbly Zera when she arrived. No way could you miss her. She turned to the platter on the counter and chose a huge white chocolate macadamia cookie. Fortification?

She'd barely swallowed her last bite and chased it with fresh coffee when she heard Zera's high-pitched voice as she came through the door from reception. *Here we go.*

Zera greeted Carol, who then informed her, "Rachel Quinn's in the kitchen, waiting for you."

Great. Thanks, Carol.

"Oh, is she? I was going to call her. Well, this'll work."

Rather than stand there looking expectant, Rachel asserted herself and moved toward the kitchen door.

Zera plastered on a smile as she approached. "Hey, look at you."

"Hi, Zera. I was in the area and thought I'd drop by so I could catch you in person."

"Let me put these away," Zera said, moving across the small kitchen and placing the syringe packages in a special box in the refrigerator. "There, done." She turned toward Rachel. "So, you have a question?"

Rachel smiled. "Questions."

Zera leaned casually against the kitchen counter and waited.

"First, I had an interesting patient from this office last Saturday. It's a convoluted story, but bottom line she had a host of remarkable symptoms right after she took her first OAinvar injection. It was quite the scene. She's not typical of our patients, and I ended up having to submit quite a long report due to her reactions. I let the office know of the situation. But basically, I wondered if you were aware of more reported adverse events recently."

"Not that I can say, off the top of my head. It's not been notable. I can check with the other educators. Are you noticing an uptick in reactions?"

"No, and as I said, that was a particularly unusual patient situation. But, if you could check with other educators, that would be great." *And you might prove to be a good source regarding their employment status.*

"Sure, I can do that."

Rachel glanced around, then asked, "So, on another point, do you know if the FDA pushed through the approval for OAinvar's indication in osteoporosis?"

"Why do you ask? Pushed through…do you mean too fast?"

Ignoring Zera's first question, she said, "Well, yeah, expedited."

Assuming a guarded look, Zera said, "I know it didn't take very long, since it was already on the market to treat inflammatory osteoarthritis. But I don't think it was unusually fast, if that's what you're asking." Her countenance changed and she smiled, "Do you want me to check on that?"

"Could you? That would be great."

"No problem." Zera regarded Rachel a bit too long, then asked, "Is there anything else?" On that note, she pushed off from the counter, ready to go.

Thankfully, she didn't press about my need to know. "No, I think that covers it. Thanks, Zera. I really appreciate it. Just let me know what you find out."

"Sure thing. Rachel. Well, I better be off. Have a good weekend."

Zera left the kitchen with dispatch and strode down the hall, taking her leave of Carol and the other staff as she went.

Rachel expelled a long sigh, composed herself, and strolled out of the office, giving a friendly wave to all as she passed by.

Glad to get that ball rolling. But where would it land?

Eleven

After a stop at Walgreens, she caught a red light. Glancing in her rearview mirror, Rachel noted a black Range Rover directly behind her, in fact rather close, but she didn't give it a second thought. She'd run to the Hen House, grab a few things, then head home.

Apparently, others had the same idea and, as she circled the large grocery store lot jockeying for a parking spot, she again noted a black Range Rover circling in the opposite direction. In that neighborhood such a vehicle wasn't rare, but still…only a coincidence or something else? Maybe, but she refused to succumb to such paranoid thoughts. Finally situated, she left her car and headed into the store, resisting an urge to glance over her shoulder now and then.

Not twenty minutes later, her shopping finished, she maneuvered out of the lot toward the street. Approaching a nearby stoplight, she glanced in her side and rearview mirrors, as was her custom. Two cars back sat a black Range Rover. *Could it possibly be?* Annoyed, and not a little uneasy, she proceeded forward when the light turned green, dividing her attention between the road ahead and her rearview mirror. Whoever it was stayed back a ways, but never turned off. *It's midafternoon, so how big a deal is this…what could go wrong?*

She knew the answer…plenty.

Deciding further assessment was in order, she suddenly turned into a convenient QuikTrip to top off her tank. Lots of people around, attendants inside. Sometimes even a cop would stop by, no matter the time of day. She got out and began fueling. No Range Rover in sight. She completed the task quickly and prepared to leave the convenience store, receipt in hand, when she noted the vehicle pull in and slowly wind its way around the aisles of pumps.

No way would she casually run into this many black Range Rovers in one afternoon over the course of her route home. Or, she had never noticed such before. Her brain told her to stay calm. Her gut told her this was no coincidence.

Trying to ignore the SUV, she motored out of the QuikTrip, and was then caught at the nearest red light not a hundred yards onto the street. How inconvenient. She'd like to have sped on her way, to have made a quick turn onto the road to her development, and maybe lose this guy. But no such luck.

Should she call Carson? What? And tell him she thought she was being tailed? He'd think she'd lost it. Or maybe not. He'd said he was up for some excitement, hadn't he?

The light turned, and she sped away, changing lanes at the first opportunity. Suddenly, the black vehicle took a right at the next intersection, heading north. Sighing relief, and feeling silly, she decided to keep this little experience to herself. At least, for the time being.

Intentionally turning her thoughts to dinner and her evening, she made her way home, and proceeded through the open security gate. This time, she noticed everything about her development. The shrubbery, her neighbors' grass, the vintage streetlamps. The quiet neighborhood appeared normal. Little traffic. *Maybe it would be a good idea to circle around again?*

Abandoning that thought, she arrived at her patio home, drove into her garage as the door lifted, and parked the car. Plucking her grocery and Walgreens bags from the front seat, she crossed the garage to her back door. Hitting the control button, she automatically turned to watch the door descend. What she also saw quickened her pulse.

A black Range Rover crawled by.

TWELVE

Saturday

Glad for the dawn of a new day, Rachel sipped freshly brewed coffee and stared at the computer screen. Her Facebook page looked weird. She couldn't access certain of her closest contacts. *What now? Another technical glitch? Yes it was, but innocent? Perhaps not.*

She had fretted all Friday evening about the probable tailing incident. Securing her home and arming the security system, she'd watched TV until late, then spent the rest of the night tossing and turning, with half the lights left on. Finally, around five a.m. she'd fallen into a deeper sleep, and awoke around seven, groggy. She didn't look forward to another night or two of that.

Perhaps she should call Carson and share with him what had happened. But something told her to resist the urge. Realizing she'd spoken to him or spent time with him each of the last four days, contributed now to a sense of reliance on him, or his strength. She didn't like that feeling, as it was one she had shunned since her divorce. Of course, he'd pursued her, too. She couldn't chastise herself for that. But he hadn't said he'd be in touch over the weekend. So, she'd soldier on and leave him alone, unless he called her. Or, unless her paranoia ballooned, or another incident occurred. Well, what about this Facebook situation? Granted, that was probably just a coincidence. Was she just looking for some rationalization to justify contacting him again so soon?

Okay, enough. She closed out her Facebook page and went to freshen her cup, mulling over various scenarios. That completed, she returned to her desk.

But clear focus alluded her, as thoughts of the past seven days intruded. What a week it had been.

That time last Saturday, all seemed in order as she had prepared to visit Linda Bates for her teaching session. No premonition, even as that scenario went south, of what the coming week held in store. No inkling that she would end up fired by Monday morning, receive calls from Carson Graham, meet Carson for drinks, have him over and allow him to review confidential reports, and end up in his office entertaining the notion of permitting some techie stranger to invade her phone app. And now on day eight of this saga, she'd suddenly developed an unexpected Facebook interruption.

Opening her social media page again, she reviewed her groups. The education company's page appeared as it usually did. She opened it and noted a number of expected 'friends'. But drilling deeper, she realized she'd been blocked from communicating with a number of others. Finally, successfully accessing one individual, she was stunned to read their comments: 'You're unfriended because of what you've done. It was inexcusable. We all strive for quality teaching, and your behavior doesn't measure up. You've harmed all of us with your actions.' She certainly didn't know that individual at all, hadn't communicated with her directly on any occasion. Was this for real, or had the company invaded the group and planted negative comments about her?

Rachel looked further. Another nurse, Susan, had just posted late Friday night. She, too, registered criticism, but at least kept it brief. 'I'm disappointed in you. Always thought you were a quality person and educator.'

She clicked on a few more. Much of the same common thread, '…lacking professional integrity…unethical, set us up for unnecessary performance reviews,' and so on. Basically, bottom line, 'you're awful,' and 'you've screwed so many of us.' Enough of looking at that stuff. She closed out the page but decided for the time being she'd not formally close her account. She might need this information in the near term.

But, no doubt, she'd been blackballed. Another new experience chalked up. And she didn't need or welcome the 'character building'.

~ ~ ~ ~

Rachel wasn't sure where she intended to go, but she'd know when she got there. Frustrated with sitting around the house, and completing her workout twice, she'd decided to take a spin around her end of town. Maybe stimulate something else to happen…like being tailed again. Then, she could probably justify calling Carson before Monday. Was she just looking for an excuse? Admittedly, maybe. In the process, she'd stop here and there for selected shopping, and work on distracting herself.

She pulled into a familiar shopping center. The clear blue sky and crisp temperature signaled fall that was just around the corner. Strolling around would put her thinking right, hopefully.

In and out of several shops, she enjoyed browsing. But, with her new status among the unemployed, she refrained from buying. She couldn't justify blowing money on clothes and accessories, especially shoes she didn't really need, in order to soothe her soul. She had taken over two closets as it was. She should probably go home and spend the rest of her Saturday cleaning out those overstuffed spaces.

As she exited the anchor store, Macy's, she glanced up and scanned the parking lot before embarking on the rather long walk to her car. And there it was. A black Range Rover occupied the third slot in, directly across from the store's entrance. Dizziness threatened, her heart pounded, as she quickly surveyed the scene. Was someone inside who'd followed her there? She hadn't noticed anything unusual as she'd strolled around. This was ridiculous, she reminded herself as she hurried off down the sidewalk. There are lots of such vehicles in this part of town and, no doubt, they have owners who regularly frequent these shops.

Unsettled, she scurried along, definitely a woman with a mission, though the purpose of which she couldn't quite explain, even to herself.

Thirteen

Monday

The remainder of Saturday and all of Sunday passed uneventfully. Well, other than the steady workings of her overactive imagination and analytical left brain. And the receipt of a formal termination letter from Advanced Education Concepts on Saturday, in which the foregone conclusion, or old news, of her firing was conveyed in a mere two terse sentences. There was nothing much to study or analyze there.

But outwardly, at least, all seemed calm. No more tailing as she picked up takeout on Saturday evening. Granted, she wasn't out and about that much on Sunday, but hadn't noticed anything unusual when she did go out, nor in her neighborhood, for that matter. Of course, the security gate remained closed during the entire weekend period. Anyone bent on terrorizing her inside the neighborhood would just have to wait until Monday morning. At least, that's what she told herself.

Refreshed, Rachel perused various internet sites for nurse educators, hitting on a few opportunities which might be good future options. She wasn't ready to fling herself at another position yet, but having information was always a good thing. Confident something would turn up soon, she closed out her search, and turned her attention to her accumulated emails. Though, none from Carson appeared in the queue.

Speaking of which, she needed to let him know what she'd

decided about the cell phone intrusion. What *had* she decided? Was she going to hand it over to Brandon, the techie, and allow him to fiddle with the app, hopefully moving it somewhere to be securely preserved? Carson seemed confident the young man could be trusted and would accomplish what he'd suggested. Still, she was hesitant. Maybe after a workout she'd make up her mind.

Just as she began deleting multiple emails, her cell chimed. Low and behold, Zera. Recalling her vacillating attitude when they'd spoken the past Friday, Rachel sensed Zera knew more than she was admitting. Why was she back in touch so soon, on a busy Monday morning, no less? Well, there was only one way to find out.

"Hello?"

"Hi there, Rachel. Busy?"

"Not too. How are things this morning?"

"Great!" Zera bubbled. "I told you Friday I'd let you know if I heard anything about OAinvar. I suppose you'd say indirectly I have."

"Okay. So, what did you learn?"

"Well, while I was discussing marketing strategies this morning with someone at M-D, they told me there's rumor of a lawsuit."

Rachel's stomach clenched. She paused, then asked, "A lawsuit?"

"Right. Apparently, several educators with Advanced Education Concepts were found to have entered data incorrectly. The M-D higher-ups are steamed. AEC may be fined for not submitting accurate data to them regarding adverse events, so they, M-D, can comply with the FDA reporting policies."

Feigning ignorance, Rachel asked, "Really? So, who might they sue?"

"I guess the educators. My source said AEC apparently felt it was better to go after the educators to try to recoup the fine before this thing went any further."

Nausea threatening, Rachel asked, "Specifically, what do you understand to be, 'this thing'?"

"Well, the incorrect reporting."

"Sure. So, that sounds serious. Did your source say what the particular error was and how many educators were involved?"

"Not specifically. They said several."

Rachel popped a nearby peppermint candy and suggested, "Perhaps they thought they'd reported it correctly and it was an innocent mistake."

"Apparently, the company doesn't think so. But, whatever, they're really mad and don't want to get caught paying big fines."

"Of course." Rachel paused, then asked, "So, did that involve maybe more adverse events occurring?"

"Not sure. They didn't say anything about that, specifically. Oh, and I couldn't get any information on how quickly OAinvar was approved, or if the process was particularly speedy."

"Of course. Well, listen, Zera, thanks for the info."

"No problem. Say, I'll keep my ears peeled and let you know if I hear anything else."

"Thanks, I'd appreciate that."

With a cordial signoff, they disconnected.

Rachel swigged a gulp of ice-cold water. How long would it be before poor Zera found out she was the pack leader…the pack of negligent nurse educators? Or maybe she was now considered a marauding lone wolf.

Rachel shelved those thoughts for the moment, and turned her attention again to her unfinished emails, and noted a new message in her inbox…from FDA.gov. Could the form possibly be here this soon? She clicked the message. Voila! There it was.

She moved down through the brief, impersonal message. An attachment containing the document caught her attention. This would be interesting to see how detailed and convoluted the government form proved to be. She clicked on it and was surprised to see an abbreviated form awaiting completion. Basically, one page, lacking redundancy or confusing instructions. No complicated information was requested. The second page was simply a signature page. She could quickly complete it, scan it, and return it that day. At least one thing could get done, and in good order.

The lawsuit issue…she would push that analysis to a later time. There wasn't a process server ringing her doorbell, yet, was there?

Fourteen

Zera scanned the ballroom before entering. A modest crowd had gathered but, no doubt, more would join within the half hour. Getting through late afternoon rush hour usually slowed a few. She walked to the complimentary bar and ordered a glass of wine. She wanted to work the room in her own way.

This particular evening, a trio of M-D Pharma company executives were hosting the usual quarterly meeting for a large cabal of regional drug reps. Typically, only the smaller metropolitan area sales force met each quarter. But that night, after a complimentary cocktail hour and an impressive plated dinner, an upper-level executive would present recent sales statistics for their three medications and communicate projections for the fourth quarter and the coming year. Occasionally, the execs introduced a quota buster to stimulate competition among the reps. They also usually added a few words regarding drug development to whet the reps' appetites for future products and sales. These gatherings were predictable and, as anticipated, one such as this, well attended. Who in their right mind would miss a free dinner and the chance to schmooze with higher ups?

After milling about, and greeting various other reps, she spotted him near the entrance. He must have just arrived. Zera took a moment before approaching to appraise and appreciate the man.

Parker Collins, thirty-eight and single, was VP for national sales. He was the evening's keynote speaker. Tall, good looking, always well turned out, he commanded the room. If he tired of his position, she felt certain he could transform into a GQ model without much effort. He certainly displayed the necessary physical qualities. It was clear several reps were maneuvering toward him. She'd take her time and wait for the right moment.

When dinner was history, and Parker's presentation neared its end, Zera had determined her strategy for cornering him. They had met before on several occasions at regional and national meetings, and he'd been fairly friendly. Some would say he had acted rather familiar. She hoped this encounter might rekindle some of that interest, if it had existed in the first place. She rose from her chair with the others after the applause died down. Parker descended the steps of the dais and lingered in front, animated and chatting with several reps. Zera saw her opportunity and approached. As she neared, he spotted her and smiled. Diplomatically dismissing the male rep who dominated his time, Parker turned to Zera.

"Well, hi there."

"Hello," she answered. "Zera Riordan."

"Yes, I remember."

"That was a great presentation. Very encouraging, excellent projections."

"Thanks. Glad you thought so. We're bullish on the sales numbers and believe next year will prove even more positive." He paused and gave her a look. "So, you're still covering part of the Kansas City region?"

"Correct. South Kansas City and parts of Johnson County. It's an active region, a good territory. I like it. The diverse practices present good opportunities. Currently, OAinvar is doing well."

"I'm glad to hear that. Despite the recent problem?"

Well, he comes right to the point. "Problem? Something you've heard?"

"Certainly. I'm surprised if you haven't. The problem which just surfaced regarding several of AEC's educators. In fact, one such educator from this area. You may know her."

"There are a couple I work with in my territory." *Better keep it general, but will he think I'm out of the loop? Not aware, not keeping up?*

He glanced around their immediate vicinity. "Well, the one I'm referring to has set the company on edge."

Not a little surprised at his directness, Zera schooled her expression. Best not react too vigorously. Best to resist offering anyone's name, and best to withhold her knowledge of any possible lawsuit. Playing that hand right then might backfire. She didn't want to put Parker off. Acting like a know-it-all might just do that.

She said, "Oh, really? That's surprising, given the ones I know. They're good educators. I'm not personally aware of any complaints against them. Trustworthy, I'd say."

"Perhaps not so much."

She gave him a quizzical look. "Oh?"

"So, one of them in particular put Advanced Education Concepts in a bind. We rely on them to do as instructed with their data, so we can report that to the FDA. If we get fined, it could tank the medication, and put the FDA surveillance people onto our other drugs. Not a good situation."

"I can see that." As an established regional rep, would he think she should have known this was going on?

He pointed a direct look at her. "Has anyone told you who it was?"

"Not yet." Which was partially true. AEC had not contacted her with any names, yet.

"Well, it just came to light a week ago. But, my understanding…they let her go."

"Amazing."

"Yeah."

Zera observed his wandering eyes as he glanced around at the thinning crowd. *Was he tiring of this conversation…of her?* She decided to take the lead and her leave. Better depart with Parker wanting to discuss more.

"Well, you've had a full day, I'm sure. I'll say goodnight. And thanks for sharing that information. No doubt, I may hear more soon." She turned toward the ballroom door.

Before she could cover three feet, Parker asked, "Say, Zera, would you like to meet for dinner some evening, maybe Friday? I'm in the area through the week. We can discuss things further, more discreetly."

She turned back and smiled. "I'd like that. Let me check my schedule and make sure it's clear."

"Sure. I'll call you tomorrow."

Realizing the VPs could access all the drug reps' numbers, she refrained from yanking out her phone to provide him that information. "Great," she replied with a smile. Mustering as much calm as possible, she turned and strolled from the ballroom.

FIFTEEN

Wednesday

As the afternoon waned, Rachel's thoughts turned to dinner. In her kitchen, she switched on her small cabinet TV for the evening news, and surveyed the refrigerator contents. And resisted the urge to make a drink. Some leftovers, a frozen meal in a bowl—both meant more for lunch than dinner. She could always make a chopped salad. Uninspired, she walked into her pantry and stood there, staring. Nothing appealed. Nor did she want to prepare an involved meal. She returned to her freezer and withdrew the Frontera chicken bowl. She'd add to its contents, make a fruit and cheese plate. Not too much strain. As she busied herself, her thoughts wandered.

Why hadn't Carson called? Well, she'd said she'd let him know her decision. Now it was Wednesday, and she hadn't held up her end of the bargain. As she chopped and sliced, her cell chimed. "There you go…all you had to do was wait," she announced to the empty room.

"Hello."

"Hi there," he answered. "How've you been?"

"Not bad, and you."

"Can't complain. I assumed you were going to call Monday. Thought I'd give you a few more days, then check in. So, here we are."

"I know. Frankly, I've struggled with indecision a bit. And a few other things have happened in the meantime."

"Shoot."

"It's more than I want to go over on the phone. Perhaps, I should schedule an appointment at your office to explain."

"I have a better idea. How about I come over this evening and you can fill me in?"

Rachel paused momentarily, then answered, "Why not? I can show you one of the issues more easily that way. So, how about seven-thirty?"

"Sounds good. I'll see you then." They disconnected.

She glanced at the wall clock—five forty-five—and resumed her food prep. This would be interesting. And, admittedly, a little exciting.

Promptly, at seven-thirty, her doorbell rang. Carson stood there in the early evening light, smiling.

She opened the door wider and stood aside as he entered.

"Hi." Surveying her, he added, "You look rested."

"A bit better last night. But that wasn't the case several days ago," she admitted.

As they turned toward her kitchen, he reassuringly patted her back.

"Coffee?" she asked.

"Sure, if you have some decaf."

"Always."

Firing up her Krups, she fixed two cups and joined him at the kitchen bar.

"So, what interfered with your sleep before last night?" he asked.

She looked at him over her cup rim. "Well, I wasn't sure if I was going to tell you this, but why not? A strange situation happened Friday afternoon after I left your office."

Concern creased his face. "What kind of strange situation?"

"I believe I was followed."

"What? Why didn't you call me then?"

"Oh, I don't know. I felt silly."

"So, did someone follow you all the way home?"

"Yes, and no."

Carson put down his cup and turned slightly on his bar stool to face her. "Go on."

"After I left your office, I grabbed a sandwich. Then I went to Dr. Reynolds' office and waited there for Zera. She planned to drop off more samples after her lunch. She arrived around a quarter to two. I asked her to look into the approval process for the medication. Had it been hurried through, and so on. Said she didn't know off the top of her head but would look into it. I also asked if other educators had recently reported an increase in adverse events. I wanted to know if she knew that. I thought it might stimulate her to tell me about the company's reporting process. I was also fishing with that question to see if she would mention my firing, or the teaching company being fined. She didn't act aware of any of that. It was a very brief conversation. On Monday when she called back, she said she'd heard about a possible lawsuit…against vagrant educators."

Carson frowned, then said, "Hold that thought. Back to the tailing, so yes *or* no, did someone follow you all the way?"

"Yes *and* no. After I finished at the office with Zera, I ran errands. When I was done at Walgreens, I noticed a Range Rover very close behind me. It was more annoying than concerning. I went off to the Hen House for a few things and noticed a black Range Rover again, cruising the parking lot while I found a spot. Not sure if it was the same one, I parked close to the door, went inside, and got what I needed. Spent about fifteen minutes there. Finished, I left and drove west, and again noticed the same car—at least, it seemed to be—behind me in the outside lane, two cars back. It was a male driver, I'm sure of that, and no one else. I proceeded along, changing lanes. I decided to top off my tank and pulled into a handy Quik Trip. No sign of him until I was leaving. Then, there he was again. Off I went with him following. At that point, I was getting anxious, and didn't want to turn onto the street coming toward my development entrance."

"Good thinking."

"Then, suddenly, the Range Rover man took a right turn at a light and headed north."

"So, you decided it wasn't a problem, just because they turned off. Maybe they'd accomplished what they wanted, harassing you. What happened after that?"

"Well…I drove home feeling a little ridiculous and pulled into my garage. But just as I lowered the door, a black Range Rover crawled by. That got my heart rate up a bit."

"I bet. Rachel, you should have called me. This doesn't sound coincidental at all. Do you know if any of your neighbors own such a vehicle?"

"No, I don't. I haven't seen one before in the neighborhood. But maybe it was someone visiting a friend. Anyway, Friday night was a bit tense and restless. But my sleep improved as the weekend unfolded. Our security gate stays closed at night and on the weekends. So that helped ease my anxieties."

"I suppose. So, otherwise, it was quiet?"

"Quiet, but not uneventful."

Carson leveled a steady look at her. "Explain, please."

"Want another cup?"

"No, I'm fine."

"Well, Saturday morning I was checking my Facebook page, the one for the company educators, and it looked weird. I scooted around and found that I, essentially, was black-balled. Several 'friends' wrote snarky, critical comments accusing me of causing all kinds of trouble for the group. Unnecessary performance reviews, etcetera. Several disparaged my character, that kind of stuff. It was upsetting, to say the least, and I stopped reading after a few posts."

She rose and rinsed out their coffee cups. Meeting Carson's gaze, she continued, "The real issue is how the other educators found out about the situation so soon, and who told them. Or did a company person go into the site, and post those comments?"

"You'll probably never find out. What happened then?"

"Disgusted, I left and did some shopping at Towne Centre to distract myself. It was a beautiful day, and I felt trapped and useless here. When I left Macy's there was a black Range Rover parked three slots from the entrance. It caught my eye immediately. I hurried back to my car, which I'd parked some distance from the store."

He asked, "No one there shadowed you?"

"Not that I noticed."

"How'd Sunday go?"

"Quiet. Well, Saturday my termination letter arrived. All of two sentences formally notifying me of what I already knew. They hadn't changed their mind."

"I'd like to see that letter, if you don't mind."

"Sure." She sipped her cooling coffee and added, "Then on Monday, Zera's comment."

Carson frowned. "The lawsuit idea?"

"Yes. She went on about some scuttlebutt she'd heard when she called the drug company about marketing strategies and my questions. According to her, there's a rumor that they're considering filing a lawsuit against the teaching company and several of the nurse educators about their reporting practices. She didn't act like she knew I was one of them. Said they want to recoup what they can in order to pay the fine they believe will be leveled on them. Actually, she knows perfectly well that M-D Pharma would be assessed the fine, not the teaching company. But, of course, they could in turn sue Advanced Education Concepts. And she didn't find out any information about other educators reporting more adverse events or OAinvar rocketing through the approval process for OP."

"OP?"

"Osteoporosis."

Carson nodded. "Okay. How reliable do you think Zera is?"

"I don't know. She impresses me as someone who's bubbly, energetic, and wants a long-term career in the industry. She seems objective, but I've only had limited contact with her."

"You want my opinion?"

"Sure."

"I'd keep my contact with her to a minimum. And I wouldn't give her any information you have about this whole reporting situation. She called and relayed the rumor of a lawsuit. Why? To be helpful? I doubt it. She may just be laying something out there to scare or signal you, may already know you're involved or at the center of the maelstrom."

"Good point, but I thought of that, too." She paused. "You want to see my Facebook page?"

"Sure." Smiling, he stood. "That might be good for a laugh. That's why I don't do social media. I couldn't stand all the attention. And I can't keep my mouth shut. I'm definitely not pc."

In her office, she signed on to her page, and showed him how to navigate the site. He assumed her desk chair and gazed at the screen.

After a moment, he said, "This is something." Then a string of comments, "Well, hell, what right do they…? For heaven's sake…You've got to be kidding." He swiveled the chair and faced her. "That's quite a diatribe. I know if it were me, I'd be furious." He paused, then asked, "Do you feel comfortable staying here alone?"

"Most of the time." She shrugged. "But I've had my moments since last Friday."

"I could stay, if you want…some company."

She held up her hands, "Oh, I can't ask you to do that."

"Yes, you can." He smiled, then became serious. "Rachel, I don't want to be underfoot or make you uncomfortable. You said you had a spare guest room. I could use that."

She stared at him for a moment. That sounded wonderful, but no way would she let on she felt that way. "Okay, I'll take you up on that. But what happens after tonight? I suspect this will persist for a while."

He smiled. "We'll figure it out."

Sixteen

Thursday

A door opened and muffled footsteps thudded the carpeted stairs. The smell of coffee hung in the air. She finished her usual morning routine and donning sweatpants and a baggy tunic top, made her way down the hall to the kitchen. Carson sat, coffee cup in hand, checking his cell phone.

"Good morning," he greeted her.

"Morning." She paused, then added, "I usually don't sleep in."

"No need now for you to rush."

"That's for sure."

"Better last night?"

"Yes."

He smiled. "So, what's on for today?"

"Don't you need to go in?"

"Yeah, but there's no time crunch. When I get there, I get there."

"Nice." She poured herself a cup and joined him at the counter. "How about yourself…was the bed comfortable?"

"Yes, very."

She paused between sips of coffee and said, "I'm ready to have Brandon try to transfer that app on my phone. When should I bring it by?"

He looked up from his cell, "We could do it later today, if you want. He's always busy, but won't make appointments for such things, so just drop by when you want, and we'll get it taken care of."

"Okay. First, some bills to pay, then I'll work out before I come by."

"Want to grab lunch before we corner Brandon, say about twelve-thirty?"

"All right. Sounds good."

Two hours later, after Carson's departure and her workout, Rachel sat at her desk and scanned emails. She was startled to see one in particular from FDA.gov. The medication information had returned this soon? She opened the message, which bore two attachments. One, her completed form, the second a two-page report. Rachel quickly read through the report, not really expecting the results given. She printed it and settled in for the second analytical read.

Amazing. It was clear from the data given that the adverse events had been underreported to the FDA. Her previous results alone, minus Linda Bates, multiplied by the total number of nurse educators she knew of would have produced more reported adverse events. The percentages just looked too low. But she obviously needed exact numbers of educators throughout the nation to be sure she could make that case. She couldn't go only on the rough numbers she'd formulated in her head. The information about the educators on the app might help. She reached for her cell to confirm she still had the functional app. It was there. No time to waste, now…she needed to move and protect that information. She jumped up from her chair, quickly closed her emails, and headed for her room to prepare for the day.

Forty-five minutes later, just as she made her way toward her kitchen door, her phone chimed. An area code she recognized as Washington, D.C. *Scam call or a pivotal communication?* Tempted to let it go to voice mail, then deciding otherwise, she put her bag on the counter and picked up.

"Hello. This is Rachel Quinn."

"Ms. Quinn. This is Judith Grayson at the FDA."

Her heart pounding, Rachel stood planted in place. First, the report so soon and now this. "Yes, hello, Ms. Grayson."

"Your request for information came across my desk last week. I was intrigued and wanted to follow up on your submission."

"Yes."

"The report is done and should be on its way to you."

"Yes, I just received it this morning. Thank you."

"Good. It was interesting for several reasons, and I think we need to discuss it. Do you have a moment?"

"Yes, I do." *Was she going to say 'yes' to everything?*

"First, let me explain my position. I sit on the FDA panel for approval of certain classes of medications. The manufacturer, M-D Pharma, has three drugs on the market, Arthremimab being their most recently approved. That came four years ago. As I believe you're aware, they sought and obtained approval for osteoporosis indication just two years ago. My panel dealt with both of those approvals. I understand, from your submitted information request form, that you are seeking information on reported adverse events. You added in the additional questions box that you also sought information on the approval process and how long it took."

"That's right."

"Well, I can tell you the answer to your second question—not long. Not long enough, in my opinion. It essentially passed across our desks and the conference room table with a glancing blow. We reviewed the very minimal information offered with the application regarding bone density studies. A modest number of osteoarthritis patients showed increases in bone densities while on the drug. I, for one, thought additional time should have been spent evaluating more studies with higher numbers before approving it for that indication. But a few of my colleagues saw it differently."

"Did pressure come from the industry?"

"You hit the nail on the head. The plain answer is, yes. Since it was already an approved drug, the additional indication approval usually doesn't take too long. But that approval was particularly speedy. There was intense pressure from the company to push it through. Minimal harms had been reported, so what was the need to slow walk it? At any rate, a few of my colleagues on the panel agreed with me, but we didn't carry the day."

Judith went on, "Your first question—the adverse reactions item—is also interesting. M-D Pharma submitted their quarterly reports in a timely fashion. But recently they've been red flagged because their data doesn't fit our statistical models."

"Models?"

"Yes. We have powered the statistics at the FDA to comb through reports submitted by drug companies. There is a percentage of post-market adverse reactions which the program expects any drug to show. If it varies from that percentage, allowing for a two-point standard deviation, the company's report generates a red flag. We then review the data manually to ascertain why it was flagged by the computer program. M-D's reporting on Arthremimab generated such a warning. In fact, just at the end of the second quarter, the end of June. So, we've been working through the manual review process since then." Judith paused, then asked, "What, in particular, was your concern about adverse events?"

"I'm a nurse educator and have taught patients how to use OAinvar for a year and a half. Several weeks ago, I had a patient who experienced multiple adverse reactions after her first injection. Entering all the data in the adverse events column of the online form extended my report to four pages. Due to a series of events involving internet interruption, I called the education company about my report. I wasn't sure it had gone through. They were distressed I had put all that information in the online form, and I ended up terminated over the issue."

"Terminated? Didn't you fill out the form correctly?"

"Oh, yes. I did. But they so much as admitted to me that they did not want it entered in the appropriate column on the online form. I was to call them and relay the data over the phone. They had apparently put that in my contract, which I didn't recall, or it wasn't there when I signed."

Judith paused on the other end. Rachel waited for her response. "Interesting. You getting fired and the reporting protocol. The drug company is required to submit all that information electronically to us. You said the education company?"

"Yes. Advanced Education Concepts."

"Just what is the setup between M-D Pharma and this Advanced Education group?"

"M-D Pharma subcontracted with them to recruit and train nurse educators. Assigned to segments of a region, we work with physicians' offices and the regional drug rep to identify patients prescribed the medication. The rep makes sure the drug is available efficiently, and we offer the medical offices and patients our educational services. The office nurses are simply too busy to spend the time required to educate individual patients who go on the drug. I worked closely with an orthopedic surgeon in my area who has an osteoporosis clinic."

"Sounds like a well-oiled machine."

"Basically, it is. Very efficient. And I believe it offers a true service to the patients, many of whom have no idea how to use such a drug."

"I'm sure. So, how did you come to work for Advanced Education?"

"I was recruited, after I reviewed their website, asked, and answered several questions. I was just curious at first. Then, as it unfolded, I became more interested, asked more questions. After that, someone from the company—I can't remember exactly who—contacted me with their recruiting pitch. I have experience in nursing education, and wanted a change of pace and more flexible hours, so it seemed a good fit for me."

"Of course. Back to this reporting issue. Am I clear in understanding that Advanced Education Concepts expected the educators to call in all their adverse events?"

"Yes, I learned that after the fact. It was okay to fill out the rest of the form online, but any reactions were to be called in. An individual answering the phone six days a week between seven a.m. and ten p.m. would take the information. Apparently, they were tasked with transmitting that data to M-D Pharma."

"Sounds like a method which could allow manipulation of the data."

"It sure does."

"Listen, I've kept you too long. I want to review what you've told me, and research a few more things. Do you still have your reports?"

"Yes, I do. All of them."

"Good. Hang on to those and secure them. I'll get back to you before too long to follow up this conversation."

"Thank you."

"And good luck to you. You've been a big help."

"You're welcome." They disconnected.

Rachel glanced at her watch—high noon. There was plenty of time to meet Carson for lunch, fill him in on the startling FDA phone call, then return to his office to get busy with Brandon.

It was good to have allies. Or so it seemed.

Seventeen

Friday

He'd secured the only remaining stool at the bar, affording a good view of the door. It was Friday afternoon in Lawrence, and the Wheel already hummed with weekend party traffic. Students, both undergraduate and graduate, the former usually younger than their stated ID age, choked the aisles and obstructed traffic between tables.

Some of his law school buddies had grabbed a booth an hour ago, now littered with pitchers and peanut shells. Periodically, they'd wave or gesture at him, but he stayed put, waiting. He didn't plan to spend the evening carousing with them, anyway. Josh Quinn had staked out his place and wasn't about to give it up.

Out of the corner of his eye he detected movement. Lowering his beer glass, he felt a presence too close on his right. He glanced at the man who stood beside him, his elbow resting on the bar. Probably in his late thirties, he wore jeans, a casual plaid shirt, and boots. Clean cut, friendly face, close-cut light brown hair, with sunglasses perched on his head. He stared at Josh, who returned his steady gaze.

"Hey, how's it going?"

The man nodded, signaled the bar tender for a beer, and turned back to Josh.

"Do I know you?" Josh asked.

"Don't think so, not yet," the stranger answered.

Josh glanced toward the door again. The party he expected, not this guy, still hadn't arrived.

The bartender returned with the man's brew. Josh stared at an ESPN Sports broadcast above the bar, but he felt the man's eyes resting on him. The next words had to come from this guy, who brought tension into his space. Maybe he'd move along, now that he was supplied.

"You Josh Quinn?" the man asked, squinting at Josh over the rim of his glass.

Obviously, this guy knew who he was, so lying was not going to work. "I am. And you are?"

"Jake."

That was doubtful. Red flags sprouted all over the countertop. Josh returned his attention to his beer and the TV monitor.

"You're second-year law," the stranger observed.

It wasn't a question. Not answering, he turned to face his interrogator, who crowded between him and the guy now perched on the stool to Josh's right.

Next guy registered his complaint at Jake, who moved a bit closer then, further invading Josh's space. Way too close. This was not a comfortable situation. Who the hell was this, anyway?

"What's your interest?" he asked Jake.

"You're from Kansas City, right?"

"What if I am?"

"And your mother's a nurse."

Alarmed then, and on guard, Josh looked directly at this Jake. "What's your interest in me or my mother?"

"Just that you need to be aware."

"Aware of what?"

"That what she did doesn't sit too well."

Done with this nonsense, Josh demanded, "What the hell are you talking about?"

Jake took a swig of beer, pulled a ten from his pocket, placing that and his half-empty glass on the bar. "Better watch your back, and hers." Without further comment, he stepped away from the bar and strolled out of the Wheel.

Josh stared after him as the guy, whoever he was, made his way through the mash of people and out into the late afternoon sun. He resisted the urge to sprint after him, confront him in the broad daylight of the Wheel's yard, and square off.

As he sat, fixated on the door, her blonde hair lit up the entrance. Courtney had arrived. She spotted him staring at the door, and made her way through the tables, stopping to acknowledge acquaintances as she approached.

"Hey," he greeted her, relinquishing his stool for her benefit.

Annoyed at Josh's apparent popularity, the man next to him threw down his money, and stood from his barstool. "Here you can have this one, too." He strode away.

Courtney, smiling, planted her bottom on the stool. "That was easy."

His concern about Jake fading fast, and the red flags regressing, he smiled back. "Do you want a beer?"

"Sure. Gosh, it's already busy."

"Yeah. Say, did you see that guy who just passed you in the door?"

"The cute older guy? Who winked at me, by the way."

Red flags re-sprouted. The jerk. Jealousy and alarm mounting, Josh said, "Jeans, plaid shirt, brown hair, and boots? Shades on his head?"

Courtney nodded. "So, what's he about?" she asked.

The bartender approached, smiled at cute Courtney, and took her order.

"I don't know yet, but he came in here, intentionally found me, and started asking questions."

"What sort of questions?"

"Statements more than questions. Name, where I'm from, who my mother is."

"Your mother? How weird."

"Yeah."

"Josh, is something wrong?"

"I don't know, but I think I'd better find out." The efficient barkeep returned with Courtney's brew.

She shrugged and took a sip of cold beer.

Josh turned and gazed at Courtney. It was Friday, and the whole weekend lay ahead. The red flags evaporated as he imagined how they could spend their time.

Obnoxious guys with fake names and stupid investigations could wait.

Eighteen

It was better than she had expected. He was already in a cozy booth situated in a corner, away from other crowded tables. Zera paused after speaking with the hostess, then crossed toward the table. Parker glanced up, smiled, and stood. Arriving at the booth, she extended her hand, which he clasped warmly, and held a moment too long.

"Glad you could join me," he said.

"Thank you. I've looked forward to it." She slid into the leather booth, and arranged her shoulder bag to her right side, not obstructing the space between them.

"Would you like a glass of wine?" he asked.

She noted he hadn't yet ordered for himself. "Perhaps, yes."

"Why don't we order a bottle as we look over the menus?"

"Sure."

A waiter approached, offered menus, inquired about drink orders, and retreated.

As they chatted and examined the menus, their waiter returned. Parker placed their wine and appetizer order, sending him on his way again. He turned to Zera.

"Has your week gone well?"

"Yes, very. And yours?"

"Good. Good. I've enjoyed tagging along with several of the other reps on their rounds, meeting some of the doctors, and getting a handle on challenges they face. We don't have an opportunity to do that very often. The Charlotte office keeps us busy."

Silence stretched between them. She was not about to broach the subject of errant educators or the lawsuit. Thankfully, their waiter returned with their wine and appetizer.

Leaning forward, he said, "So, as we were saying Monday evening…the issue of OAinvar reporting."

Zera sipped and nodded.

"To be blunt, this reporting issue is turning into a big problem. The one nurse educator who went rogue with her electronic forms. And likely others. It seems Advanced Education Concepts apparently wasn't watching closely enough. Sources at headquarters have informed us that the educator completed the patients' forms online, including using the adverse events column. And she'd been doing it that way the entire time she'd been teaching, which has been a couple of years. To cover their asses, AEC protested that they'd written that into all the contracts, that the educators were to call in any reactions to the help desk. The individual manning the phone desk would then complete the entire form and transmit it to us electronically. I'm told she said she didn't know that was in her contract."

Zera tilted her head, listening intently. She sipped wine as Parker went on.

"This whole thing has caused a real mess. We rely on accurate reporting to comply with FDA rules."

Accurate reporting? So, what's our definition of accurate?

Parker went on, "If we screw that up, big fines could be levied against the company and invite ongoing FDA scrutiny." He paused. "You did say you knew her fairly well, right?"

Wait a minute…she hadn't said anything about anyone in particular Monday evening. "Yes, I do know several educators fairly well."

"So, what can you tell me about her? Does she stay in close contact? Or does she go off the reservation on a regular basis?"

No longer able to remain passive, Zera put down her wine glass and leaned back.

"Which one exactly are you referring to?"

Parker gazed at her for a moment too long. He wasn't believing this, she could tell.

"Specifically, one Rachel Quinn."

"Oh, yes. I know Rachel. She's an RN, a good nurse, and a great educator. She, in fact, has helped us train other nurse educators. She has a background in nursing education, and prior to that worked in a hospital setting for many years. Our doctors like her, too."

"Go on. Anything else?"

"I'm shocked to hear that her termination is true. It just doesn't fit."

"She hasn't mentioned it to you?"

"Actually, no, she hasn't. She and I spoke, though, last week about several questions she had on OAinvar."

"Questions she had? That would have been after her termination. What did she want to know?"

Why is Parker so obsessed with Rachel's reporting and firing? So what if she filled out the AE column herself. "She asked whether we noticed an uptick in reported adverse reactions for OAinvar. I told her I wasn't aware of an increase. Then, she asked if the FDA approval process had been particularly speedy. I told her I didn't think so."

A brief shadow flickered across Parker's face.

Zera added, "Then I told her I'd check into it for her. She said she'd appreciate that."

Parker gazed at Zera for a few moments, his face softening, just as their waiter and another server arrived with their main course. Suspending their discussion, he turned his attention to his plate, which was a relief. His scrutiny seemed rather intense.

She'd expected this dinner would address the issue, but had hoped it would veer in a more social direction. Or perhaps it would steer toward career advancement. Perhaps an opportunity for a different region. Maybe even Dallas? She'd always thought the Metroplex would be a good move. Her thoughts swirling, she turned her attention to her meal, as well. Time passed as they ate, chatted about the menu and new restaurants in the area, touched on Kansas City sports and other attractions. Rachel and her egregious behavior had been tabled, temporarily.

Their meals done, the waiter returned to inquire of possible dessert choices. Both declined, but Parker explained they would like to finish their bottle of wine. Left alone again, he resumed his discussion of the Rachel issue.

"Zera, I'm concerned, as are others, about this situation with the Quinn woman. As I've said before, our reporting must be scrupulous. If questions arise, the FDA might flag not only Arthremimab, but the other drugs we manufacture and sell. You understand, I'm sure, how that would affect M-D Pharma." He scooted a bit closer, stretching his long arm along the back of the booth, his hand resting behind her neck.

"Of course." Warmth suffused her middle, her spine tingled.

He smiled, and continued in a confidential tone, "And the fines I spoke of earlier, they can be considerable. We've made so much progress just in the past five years, we don't want to run into a problem. It's allowed us to bring more reps on board, such as yourself, and to enhance our R and D division." His hand barely grazed the back of her neck as he finished speaking and rearranging himself in the booth. More tingling and near dizziness threatened to undo her, or was it the wine? "More new drugs in development, all of that." He threw her that million-dollar smile.

To say she was concentrating on his comments would be a lie. This man was irresistible, and he knew it. But what did she care if he was sincere? Being there with him, right then, was fine. So fine. She said, "That's the whole point, I'm sure."

"Exactly."

His intense gaze, his clear blue eyes—appearing as mere liquid pools of cool water—nearly mesmerized Zera. *Water or wine…of which one to partake?* She gracefully reached for her wine and took another sip, trying desperately to steady herself.

"It's possible this thing won't turn out so bad after all. If we all work together to reset the reality."

"I'm listening." Which she wasn't.

"It might be beneficial, I'm thinking, if we had more information from the field. And you could be just the person to assist with that."

"Information from the field?" *Was he asking her to spy?*

"Exactly. If you stay in touch with this Rachel Quinn, you could assess what she's doing, who she's talking to, that sort of thing." His hand slipped down, giving her right shoulder a little rub. Which very nearly precipitated her dropping her wineglass. "We never know when a bit of information, however trivial it seems, might be helpful."

She very deliberately, carefully, placed her wineglass on the table. "I can see how that might be worthwhile. But I don't run into her now, since she's been let go."

"You're a smart woman. I'm sure you can figure out how to contact her. Call up and express concern for her situation, let her talk. She may tell you something about any efforts she's making to investigate what happened." He paused and smiled. "She's a smart woman, too, and is probably not sitting around nursing her wounds. Maybe find out who she's talking to."

Zera returned his smile.

He pivoted. "You know, I'm sure you like Kansas City. Most people I've met here seem to want to stay, make it their permanent place. But there may be other opportunities which could prove very exciting, in a bigger region, for instance. Reps move in and out of some of the other larger, more mobile cities. Denver and Dallas are two which come to mind. Maybe even advancement to a higher position in Charlotte."

Zera's heart pounded, her smile now permanently plastered. *Now, he's talking.*

"You might find that idea appealing."

Appealing? Fantastic was the word! She offered, "Something will work out. I can make contact with her now and then, without raising her suspicions, I'm sure."

He smiled, "I'm sure you can, too." Pulling back, he asked, "Ready to go?"

Go where? "Yes."

They both slid out of the booth in separate directions. He closed the distance between them, and placing his hand on her back, guided her through the tables to the massive front door. Once out in the cool September evening, he enveloped her hand in his. Large, warm, and protective. Zera couldn't have planned a better outcome.

"Why don't we leave your car here?" he suggested. "There's a nice bar at the Sheraton, and I feel like a drink. Want to join me?"

"Why not?"

Nineteen

Saturday

Rachel stood in her walk-in closet and stared at her clothes. Most of these things she'd had for a while and was tired of them. But they were her style, and God forbid she'd throw away something she liked just because it wasn't the current trend. Trendy, she was not. Rifling through a few blouses, she settled on several possibilities for that evening, still not convinced she didn't need to make an emergency run to a favorite store. *Remember now, you're officially unemployed.*

This time Carson's invitation was not so off-hand. He was making intentional moves now, and she wasn't sure she felt ready for such a change. There was a bigger project at hand which required her clear focus. Having a burgeoning new relationship was not the priority. But this wasn't really a new relationship, was it? They'd known each other for five years. And a definite history existed between them, one that wasn't altogether pleasant due to all those previous complicated circumstances.

But, oh well, the project for the next few hours was settling on something appropriate to wear. Then enjoying the evening and conveying the right signals. Admittedly, she wasn't sure which signals she wished to send. Retreating from her closet and turning on her shower, she began to prepare.

At precisely six-thirty her doorbell rang. Rachel took her time answering. She'd finally chosen her favorite cream silk blouse, black slacks, and a colorful dressy jacket, devoid of beads or sequins, though. She was determined to avoid a matchy-matchy look. Carson was taller than her by more than six or so inches, giving her easy leeway on her heel height. As she turned the knob, she wondered why these thoughts even entered her mind.

"Hi," she greeted him.

"Hi."

"Come on in." Which he did.

"You look fantastic."

"Thank you, and you as well," she countered, triggering an appreciative smile from him.

"Would you like a drink before we leave?"

"No, the reservation is for seven. Even though they're fairly relaxed there, I think we should go on over. We can enjoy cocktails before dinner."

"Sounds fine." As she fetched her envelope bag, and turned toward him, he withdrew a small rectangular box from his inside pocket and extended it toward her with a smile. "What do you have there?" she asked, knowing full well he offered her a gift. *How this is accelerating!*

"Something I saw in the window."

"Oh, really?"

"Go ahead and open it."

She slid the thin silver ribbon from the glossy, black box and removed the lid. Nestled in store-monogrammed tissue rested a thin, sterling silver cuff bracelet. Just her style. She looked up.

"Oh, Carson, it's beautiful. But you really shouldn't have."

"I know. But I wanted to. It seemed just right for you."

"I can't deny it's what I like. Thank you." Donning it, she smiled. "Shall we go?"

"Definitely."

~ ~ ~ ~

The hostess guided them to a private booth, away from the hub bub of server traffic, obviously pre-arranged by Carson. They settled in, placed their cocktail orders, and scanned the menus.

Their waiter came and went as necessary, refraining from overly solicitous intrusions.

Folding his menu and looking up, Carson asked, "So, how have things gone since you left my office Thursday afternoon?"

"No changes since then. It's been quiet."

"Any further harassing cars roving around? I figured you would call if that happened again."

"Not that I noticed, which is reassuring."

The staff returned with their drinks, and after placing their orders for the main course and wine, they resumed discussion.

"I was pleased Brandon could transfer your app to a different platform. It'll be more secure."

"Yes, I'm just glad it's done. With the possible tailing, and Facebook posts, I began wondering if my computer would end up hacked."

"Reasonable concern."

"It's certainly possible the posts were real, not fake insertions from someone at AEC. But these days you never know how technologically aggressive your opponent may be."

"True."

"Of course, you know that. How silly of me to go on like this."

"Not silly. It's been my business for years now to stay on top of tech advances. We can't provide security without staying ahead of the other side, or at least keeping pace with them. It's challenging, but we have equally, or more, talented people working with us."

She nodded and sipped her cocktail. Best to go slow with the spirits.

"So, any more from the FDA woman? Judith, was it?"

"Right. Judith Grayson. No, nothing more yet. Her quick response was quite remarkable, I thought."

"Not typical of a federal bureaucracy, for sure."

"Um, hum. She was so up front about the approval process. Didn't mince words. I'm still rather surprised she admitted her reservations about the additional approval for use in osteoporosis. I told you several panel members also agreed with her motion to extend the period while they examined more research or took the opportunity to recommend additional studies. But they were overruled by other colleagues on the panel."

"I recall you said. But the drug's done so well."

"As far as we know. However, if the reporting is skewed, then they're operating with flawed data and patient information. It's a potentially huge market out there and getting bigger by the day with the aging population, both men and women. The pressure on the FDA is enormous, and they always want to have accurate side-effect data."

"I can see that. So, how did you two leave it? You didn't say. Is she going to stay in touch, or wait for you to contact her again?"

Rachel noted two waiters approaching with their meals. She finished before they were within earshot.

"She's going to check into a few things and get back to me."

"Sounds good."

Their meals then in front of them, they paused to pour wine and settled in to enjoy their food, curtailing further serious discussion.

Later, over dessert, Carson redirected to her situation when he said, "I've done a bit of digging myself. I hesitated to tell you this earlier, but decided withholding it doesn't benefit either of us, or your issue."

She looked up from her crème Brule and decaf coffee. "Oh, you have?"

"Yes. It so happens an acquaintance of mine, our senator Mike Taggart, is close friends with a key senator from Virginia. Senator Jackson, 'Jack', Stanwood who sits on the Senate HELP committee which oversees the FDA."

"HELP Committee? That's an interesting acronym. Sounds fitting."

"Yeah. That's Health, Education, Labor and Pensions. He's apparently well acquainted with this Judith Grayson. They've worked together on oversight activities and hearings. Taggart maintains Jack's a decent man who is concerned things are done right. Apparently he keeps lobbyists at arm's length. At any rate, Taggart suggested you contact Stanwood's office, if this thing gets overheated."

"Did he define, 'overheated'?"

"No, but if you're increasingly uncomfortable, or anything else happens, you might want to consider doing that."

"Okay, but let's back up for a moment. So, how do you know our Senator Taggart? You said he's an acquaintance of yours?"

"Yeah. I've known him since college. He's a fraternity brother, was a good guy then and still is, apparently. I pegged him as ambitious but didn't think he had aspirations toward politics. Not surprising, I guess, when I look back. If I recall correctly, he was set to become our chapter president, but got beat out by a guy in the house who was a legacy."

"So, you've stayed in touch?"

"Yeah, our sons were pledges together, and we'd visit at fathers' weekends, games, all that. And occasionally I'd run into him when he was home from Washington."

"This is his second term, right?"

"Yeah, and I think he wants to run for a third, but he hasn't confirmed that."

"Back to the issue and his suggestion that I might contact this Senator Stanwick…"

"Stanwood, Jack Stanwood."

"Okay, Stanwood…that seems a little over the top, calling a senator."

"Perhaps, although people do it all the time. First, you'll probably deal with a staffer. They relay the message to the politician, then usually the staffer returns with some information. Occasionally, if the issue is a hot button for them, the legislator will call back."

"How exciting."

"Can be." He smiled.

"I'll think about it."

"And my forensics guy is still working on your contract. He should be done with it next week."

"Good."

Finishing their desserts and coffee, and having put the wine bottle aside, Carson suggested they leave. He requested and took care of the check, then asked that the unfinished bottle be recorked for later. Escorting her through the restaurant and out into the cool evening, Rachel wondered what was in store from there. It didn't take long to find out.

"Would you like to catch a movie or go back to your place?"

"Are you asking yourself over, since we've missed most of the movies' start times?"

"I guess I am," he said, flashing a boyish grin.

TWENTY

It didn't take long to arrive at her neighborhood gate. But with a swerve, Carson made a U-turn and headed in the opposite direction again.

Instinctively her right hand went for the grab handle, the so-called 'Oh, Jesus grip'.

"Carson! What on earth are you doing?" She shot him a look.

"Being careful." He added, "I've kept an eye on someone for about the last three miles hanging tough back there."

"What? Someone's tailing us?"

"Not sure but could be. I'm going to cut through one of these neighborhoods and see if I throw him off, or we'll know what he's up to fairly soon."

"What kind of vehicle?" She strained to look back over her left shoulder.

"A black Range Rover."

Alarmed, her pulse whooshing in her ears, she couldn't contain her anxiety. "Oh, pleeease…not again."

"Don't worry. I'll handle this. If this is what I think it is. Open my glove compartment."

Respecting his firm tone, Rachel released the grab handle, and did as requested. She quickly saw the object of his interest. "You have a gun in here."

"Yes, I do. And I'm permitted."

"Well, that's just great. What do you expect will happen?"

"You never know. The lock's on. Hand it to me."

Gingerly plucking the firearm from the small compartment, she handed it across the console. He placed it on the floor under his seat. "Now hold on," he advised.

She placed a steadying left hand on the console and grabbed the assist grip again with her right.

Suddenly braking, he turned left abruptly at the next corner, and sped up a short hill into a heavily forested neighborhood. Passing one short block, he chose the next corner and took a left there, then made another left turn into a secluded, quiet cul-de-sac. He pulled into the driveway of a darkened house and threw the car into park, killing the lights.

She huffed out a breath and relaxed her grip. "So, we're going to do what? Sit here until he shows up?"

"Maybe."

"What if the owner comes home, or turns on the lights and sees us here?"

"I know them. They're out of town."

"So, their neighbors may think something's going on and come check or call the police."

"The more the merrier in this situation."

"And if he doesn't find us?"

"We'll leave and make our way back to your place."

"Sounds like you've got a plan for any contingency."

"Pretty much."

They sat still for nearly ten additional minutes without speaking. It seemed like ten hours, with Carson watching the mirrors and scanning the environment at both ends of the street.

Rachel kept an eye on the street to her right and decided the best policy—keep quiet.

Apparently finally satisfied, he put his car in gear and slowly backed out of the driveway. Coming to the first corner, he glanced up and down the residential street, hung a right, and retraced their route. Coming to the next stop sign, he assessed the through street and took a right.

Covering the rather short distance to her gated development, they drove in silence. Carson kept his eyes peeled the entire trip. Anxious, Rachel found herself monitoring her side mirror. When they had proceeded through her security gate and taken the first curve to the right, he asked her to raise her double garage door, and quickly drove his car into the empty second space. He cut the engine; she hit the remote and down came the door. That night, her rare custom of carrying an extra door opener in her purse had proved advantageous. The first time in years she'd had to use it. Well, there's always a first time.

They exited his car, him toting his firearm, and entered her house through the kitchen door. Tonight, her sanctuary didn't feel quite so secure. Glad Carson had come in with her, she asked, "So, what do you think?"

Still serious and quiet, he said, "I'm not sure. But it appeared that SUV was on our tail. His movements, speed, all seemed to point to that."

"The alarming thing is, if it's the same person, he knows where I live. He drove past here Friday afternoon, a week ago."

"Right."

Regarding him for a few moments, she moved to her coffee maker and asked, "Would you like some coffee?"

"No, but I could use a glass of ice water." Playing cat and mouse obviously had made him thirsty. He placed his firearm on her counter, removed his jacket and tie, and made his way to her adjoining family room, dropping onto the sofa. "Your security gate helps."

She eyed his gun as ice clunked into his glass. It looked so cold, so industrial…the weapon, not the ice. "For sure. Well, at least at night and on weekends." The water prepared, she ignored the firearm and joined him.

"I noticed your porch light on when we pulled in. Do you have other lights around the property?"

"Yes. And they come on automatically, triggered by the dark and motion."

"Good. And you use your alarm system at night?"

"Yes. And sometimes during the day when I'm gone."

"I'd use it all the time. Do you have a weapon?"

A weapon? Maybe a good right kick. "No. Other than my kitchen knives, I don't own weapons. No fireplace poker either."

He nodded. A small smile creasing his face, he asked, "Can you wield a mean knife?"

"Never have for that purpose."

"It's probably better that way. Knife fights can get kind of mean and messy."

After a long drink of water, he leaned back on the sofa, apparently recovered. "What do you have to watch?"

Really? How can he be so casual? We'll just forget what could have happened and settle in for a good movie? With our favorite pistol on the counter, at the ready.

"Let's check out Netflix."

"All right."

As she pointed her remote at the screen, he closed the gap between them and wrapped a protective arm around her shoulder, pulling her back into the cushions. "And I'm not leaving you alone here tonight, so get used to it."

"Are we 'figuring this out'?"

"That's just what we're doing."

Twenty-One

Sunday

It was time to retrieve Saturday's mail, which she had ignored while distracted by her dinner date preparations the previous afternoon. With half the day already spent, she finally remembered to go check.

Rachel strolled to her locked mailbox in the clustered brick structure one door down and fetched the small pile of various magazines, ads, and a few envelopes. It was such a beautiful fall afternoon, she thought she might just indulge in a good, long walk before Sunday night supper and football. And maybe Carson would call.

He had spent the night Saturday but took to the guest room again. She hadn't insisted, nor was she disappointed. He certainly was behaving as a gentleman, protective, and mentioning several times he didn't want her to feel pressured. Admittedly, had he persisted otherwise, she suspected she would not have resisted.

At her kitchen counter, she sorted and tossed junk mail. A plain envelope caught her eye. Likely a solicitation letter, she was tempted to toss it along with the other pieces. Better to open it, though, and make sure it wasn't something. As she reached for her handy letter opener in the drawer, her cell chimed with an incoming call. She picked it up and saw the familiar number.

"Hi there, Josh, how're you?"

"Good…good."

"You're calling earlier than usual." She put down the letter opener and strolled to a handy bar stool. She hadn't spoken with her son in several weeks, sensitive to how busy he undoubtedly was with the start of another academic year.

"I had some time this afternoon, and thought I'd check in. Going to study this evening with a group."

"So, how's Courtney?"

"Great. Loves her senior year and living out of the Theta house in her new apartment."

"Good. So, how's it going for you? Tough courses?"

"Yeah, a couple are challenging."

A lull developed. Rachel sensed Josh had called with a specific agenda and hoped it didn't involve his father.

"Mom, so, I just wondered how you were doing?"

"Hon, I'm doing fine. A few work challenges, but, you know, that's how it goes sometimes."

"Work challenges? What's going on?"

"Oh, it's nothing you need to worry about. It'll get straightened out, I'm sure."

"I disagree. I may need to worry about it."

"What are you talking about? I don't need to burden you with my work situations."

"No. But someone else has."

"Josh, what do you mean?"

"Mom, I was sitting in the Wheel Friday afternoon, minding my own business, when some stranger came up and said some things."

"Said what things, Josh?"

"First, he correctly identified me. Then confirmed I'm second-year law and from Kansas City. After that, he mentioned your name."

"My name? Who was this guy, Josh?"

"I don't know. Said he was Jake. A fake name, I'm sure."

"Jake? What happened then?"

"He said I should watch my back, and yours as well."

Stunned, Rachel froze, her heart pounding, a wave of queasiness welling up.

"Mom?"

"Yeah, I'm here."

Josh explained further, "He knew you were a nurse, and that you'd done something that, quote, didn't sit too well. What did you do, Mom?"

"Did he say anything else?"

"No, he left. Are you involved in something serious?"

"Yes, but no, not the way he made it sound." She paused for a moment. "I might as well tell you, I was fired from the teaching company I worked for. Said I didn't complete an online form correctly, which might cause them a real problem with the FDA."

"So, you've hacked off the feds?"

"No, I don't think so, but I really don't know for sure, yet. The company said they might have to pay a hefty fine."

"What's happened so far?"

Considering how much she should reveal, she said, "In a nutshell, I had a strange patient in a teaching session two weeks ago. I entered her numerous side effects in the appropriate part of the online patient report form. Had an internet interruption that Saturday evening due to a bad storm, so I checked on it the following Monday, and caught hell for having used the online form, and for not calling them first."

"Mom, you may need some legal advice. Did you know you were to call them? Did you have an employment contract?"

"Yes, Josh, I did…have a contract. But there's a possibility that wasn't in the document when I signed it. And no, I was not aware I was to call in each patient's symptoms to a phone jockey. So, anyway, I've been cut off from their website, and blackballed on their Facebook page."

"Have you called Dad?"

"Heavens, no."

Her son remained silent on the other end, then said, "Back to this guy at the Wheel. He looked the military type, Mom. His words about watching our backs sounded threatening. Has anything else come up?"

"Oh, a couple of times, I thought someone was following me. But I'm sure it's just my imagination working overtime." She wasn't about to tell him Carson Graham's imagination had kicked into high gear, as well.

"Mom…"

"What?"

"Maybe I need to come home and stay for a while."

"No, Josh, I don't want you to do that. Driving back and forth daily to Lawrence is a real grind. Please."

"I'm worried. Do you have someone who can stay with you or hang around?"

"Matter of fact, I do."

"Who?"

"A person I've known for a while. It'll be okay, Josh. I'm a big girl and can handle myself."

"Is this a guy, Mom?"

"Do you have a need to know?"

"Okay, so it is. Did he just materialize out of thin air when this started? Maybe you should question his motives."

"Now, your imagination is working overtime, son. Listen, I'll keep you informed. And if I feel in danger or things change, you'll be the first to know. But, please, don't pull your father into this. I really can't deal with him right now."

"All right. But don't let this go too far before you get help. I can come any time."

"Josh, I appreciate your concern. I'll keep you in the loop, promise."

"Who is he, Mom?"

"Later, Josh."

And Rachel hung up on her son. The tables finally turned, after so many times he'd 'accidentally disconnected' at her motherly probing. A small smile curved her lips.

Which quickly vanished at the thought of some guy sauntering into the Wheel, specifically finding Josh, referring to her and The Situation. Not comfortable, to say the least. Carson probably *would* be interested in all that.

She turned her attention, then, to the throwaway mail.

Queasy didn't adequately describe the waves which threatened to reproduce her lunch or send her running. Maybe she should take the letter and go lay on the floor in the bathroom until this passed, like Linda Bates had. Stuck on the bar stool, Rachel stared at the strange message.

She couldn't read the postmark clearly. No return address. A typed letter from an unknown person. Unsigned. But the message was clear. They knew where Amanda was, away at school for her first year of college. Referred to her dorm. Informed Rachel of several of her classes.

She dropped the letter and stared out the large window beyond her dining table. Now, it was getting serious. The afternoon sun receded behind a bank of advancing clouds. Fall thunderstorms pushing through—an approaching cold front—portended a noisy, stormy evening. Could she weather the coming storm? She had to. Essential that she make two phone calls, she rose and took a deep breath.

Ten rings, no answer. Tightness gripped Rachel's chest. Her breath caught. Where was Amanda? Anywhere. She could be anywhere. She practiced slow deep breathing, and reprimanded herself for overreacting. A freshman college girl might be shopping, eating out with friends, studying with her phone muted, or for heavens' sake, at the grocery store. Or taking another call, ignoring her mother's, or out with some strange guy, or…gone missing!

She had to get a grip so she could think straight. Dialing the second number, she sat down at her table, head in hand.

Twenty-Two

"I'll be right over."

She re-cradled her phone, a wash of relief warming her. But a burning headache threatened.

After trying Amanda three more times, and leaving messages, she had decided to call Carson, Josh's cautionary words about his possible motives notwithstanding. This situation had taken a jump shift and, obviously, it wasn't her imagination or paranoia.

Not fifteen minutes later, her doorbell rang. Carson stood on the porch wearing a worried expression, and clothes he'd obviously been in all day—comfortable faded jeans, flannel shirt, and sockless old Dockers. Behind him, she saw lightning flash in a distant cloud bank. She opened the storm door and he entered without further invitation.

He turned and looked at her. "What's going on?"

She led the way into the kitchen. "Josh called earlier and told me a tale about some guy who approached him at the Wheel in Lawrence on Friday."

"Go on."

"Said the guy came up, confirmed Josh's identity and that he's a law student from Kansas City. He then mentioned my name and knew that I'm a nurse. And...he told Josh I had done something that 'didn't sit well', and that we should watch our backs. Then, just like that, he left."

"Did he give a name?"

"Yes, Jake, but Josh is sure it's fake."

"All right. So, what's this other business with your daughter?"

She moved to another counter, retrieved the letter, and handed it to him. "This came in my mail yesterday. I just opened it today."

Carson scanned the brief message then leveled a look at Rachel. "Okay. The key here is to stay calm."

"Easier said than done." She walked away.

"Of course. So, you called Amanda and couldn't reach her?"

"That's right. Total of four times." She turned back to face him. "Carson, maybe we should call the police."

"Not so fast. She may not be missing. We should give it a few more hours."

Alarmed at his calm, she snapped, "If someone's snatched her, she may not have a few more hours!"

Carson closed the space between them and drew Rachel into his arms. "Believe me, if that's the case, they probably want something in return and will contact you. Soon. This likely wouldn't function as some random abduction."

"Or it could be."

Rachel pulled back and scanned his face. Any trace of insincerity? Dark motives? His serious eyes fixed on her, she looked away. She didn't trust herself to detect any subtleties. Easing from his embrace, she made her way to the couch and sank into the cushions.

"I don't know what to think right now."

"Okay, let's do this. You try Amanda again, and I'll order some take out. We need to eat, then we can develop a strategy. What sounds good?"

"Nothing."

"Granted, but you have to eat something."

"No Mexican, no pizza, you decide. I thought I was going to lose it a while ago. My lunch, that is."

Two hours, six placed calls, and one dinner later, they sat on the couch, waiting. The fireplace lit the room, save for a lamp in the corner. The occasional low rumble of thunder punctuated their conversation, the worst of the approaching storms due soon.

Exhausted, Rachel stared at her phone. Carson had taken over—making coffee, bringing her a wrap, holding her, and advising next moves. She'd made one decision—to not call Josh back that night until she knew more. Otherwise drained of energy, Rachel worked to push aside morbid thoughts, and focused on the conversation she'd have later with Amanda. If she had to stay up all night, she would. Who was she kidding? There would be no sleep, anyway.

Carson broke the silence. "I think I'll stay."

She certainly wasn't going to fight such an offer. Staying alone that night would be unbearable, at best. "Okay."

"And there's someone I'm going to contact, no matter how the night goes."

"And who is that?"

"A friend. He's former FBI…"

"Oh, Carson, is that really necessary?"

"He has a private security firm now. I think you and your kids need some coverage. They're discreet, good at what they do. I've had to use them a few times for executives involved in sensitive security issues."

Rachel stared at Carson. This man has had experiences she'd never envisioned.

"Unless you strongly object, I'd like to give him a call."

"Okay, I guess. If you think it's necessary."

"I do, Rachel."

He rose from the couch and pulled out his cell. It was nine-thirty p.m. Walking across the room to the hall, he made the call.

"I thought you meant after tonight," she called after him. Carson didn't acknowledge her paltry objection.

Ten minutes later, he returned and sat down next to her. "Done."

"Just like that."

"Yes. He'll get back with me in the morning and work out more details. He knows where your kids are and is sending people in both directions now. And someone to hang around here."

She stared at him. "Do we need that tonight…with your gun-fighting skills?"

"Backup never hurts." He pulled her toward him in a warm embrace. "It'll be okay."

"That's what I must focus on." She looked up at his calm face. Gazing down at her, he lowered his head, covering her mouth with a warm kiss. Surprised, and overwhelmed, she leaned in, returning his passion with hers.

Shortly after midnight, the noisiest of the storms having passed, she quietly slid from her bed, donned a light robe, and tiptoed from the room. She didn't want to disturb Carson. He slept quietly beside her, apparently spent after their two earlier rounds of frantic lovemaking. Sex like she'd not had in years. She had not slept a wink after that, lying quietly beside him as he drifted off, listening to the rain and thunder, her thoughts churning. What had she just done, putting this man in her bed? And where was her precious Amanda?

Out of earshot of her bedroom, she dialed Amanda again. After five rings, her daughter answered. "Mom, what are you doing calling so late?"

Rachel couldn't speak. It took all she could muster just to say her daughter's name. "Amanda."

"Yeah, that's me. You sound strange. Is something wrong?"

"I wasn't sure. I thought it was. It's been a long evening."

"Mom, what's going on? Did something happen to Dad? Is Josh okay?"

"Yes, honey, yes. I mean Josh is okay, but I don't know about your father. Are you okay?"

"Mom, I don't know what you just said. I'm fine, but I've got to finish studying for this Calculus test tomorrow, so I don't want to hang on the phone."

Warm relief surged; her head swam. She gripped the kitchen counter to steady herself. "Sure. Just couldn't connect with you earlier and I began to worry."

"Mom, I'm in college now, and busy. You know."

"Yes, honey, I know. Well, good luck with your test tomorrow. Let me know how it goes."

"I will, Mom. Now get some sleep."

"Sure. Love you, Amanda."

"Love you, too. Now, bye." And her daughter hung up.

Rooted in place, Rachel shivered. Her heart pounded. Moments later, two warm arms encircled her.

"Reached her?"

Rachel looked up at Carson and nodded.

Taking her shoulders, he propelled her back through the hall to her room and the edge of the bed. Assuming the other side, he pulled her down beside him, wrapped his bare arms around her. "It's going to be fine."

Without a word, and wide awake, she expelled a deep breath and relaxed for the first time in hours.

TWENTY-THREE

Monday

There was no question who was calling. And she didn't relish any conversation she would have with the person on the other end. "Nelson, why are you calling this morning?"

"What are you up to, Rachel?"

Whoever said Mondays were dull? "I am not up to something, and I don't see that it should be your concern."

"I am always concerned about you, Rachel."

"Nonsense. So, let's move on. I'm busy, and we can have this discussion some other time."

"Josh called."

That stopped Rachel in her tracks. What had Josh told his father? The last thing she needed right then was her ex jumping in the middle of this whole mess. "Then tell me about Josh's call, and I'll tell you if he's relayed the right information."

"Okay. He called last night, said he'd had a strange conversation with you in the afternoon. That you're involved in some predicament, that he was threatened because of it while at the Wheel on Friday, and that some man is hanging around."

"Oh, so that's the issue. Some man hanging around."

"No, Rachel, that's not the issue. But, the whole thing, whatever it is that you're involved in, is the issue at hand. I won't sit on the sidelines if the kids are threatened."

"Look, Nelson, I don't need to explain myself to you…"

"Yes, you do, if our kids are involved," he shouted.

"Lower your voice, or I'll hang up right now. And I'll remind you, they are of age and can do whatever they wish, despite you or me. Your fatherly concern is commendable, but I'm not involving them in some nefarious activity I may be engaged in, which I'm not." She wished that were a truer statement. "They are protected and safe."

"So, what do you mean by *protected?* Seems, Josh thinks someone's been tailing him since last night. Called me again this morning reporting that. Is that what you mean?"

"Nelson, really. They're safe." At least, she hoped they were.

"Rachel, Josh thinks you may need legal help."

"Josh is a second-year law student, Nelson. He thinks everyone needs legal help, just to cross the street. So, you're now taking the opinion of your twenty-four-year-old son, who's just begun studying tort law? Come on."

"Okay, okay. But I warn you, Rachel, if you've involved the kids in some situation that's endangering them, you'll find yourself needing legal help, and not mine."

"Goodbye, Nelson." She hung up with no small measure of satisfaction. Deep breaths in and out—and a count to ten—should do it.

Now, on to more important things. At least she knew the kids were under appropriate surveillance. Hopefully. Nelson's call had confirmed that, at least for Josh. Hopefully. Carson seemed to know a number of effective people in strategic places. Coincidence? Perhaps. But maybe something which could stand more exploration, and explanation.

Rinsing her lunch dishes, Rachel glanced out her kitchen window as the tan, late model sedan crawled by. There they were. Somewhat reassuring. She'd have to go out for her mail in a while and see where they parked. Probably in the small turnout just around the corner. Guest parking in her subdivision sure came in handy, for more than just social reasons. It was certainly better than a car lurking at the curb next door. And no black Range Rover in sight. Her cell chimed, interrupting her thoughts. Amanda.

"Hi hon, how was your test?"

"Hi Mom. It went fine. Think I did well."

"Good. So, your week's getting off to a good start."

"Maybe." Rachel heard music in the background. "That's not why I called."

"Okay?" Had she been in touch with her father, too?

"Mom, I think someone is following me around."

"What do you mean, Amanda?"

"Well, when I left the dorm this morning it looked like someone was waiting in a car in our parking lot. I was walking with a friend to my first hour, the test, so I didn't worry too much. She went off to another building, but I could swear that a guy on foot stayed on me until I went in the Noyce Center. Honestly, I was sort of freaked. After my exam, I left Noyce and I'm sure he picked me up again when I got to the main walk."

"Can you tell if he's still hanging around?"

"I'm not sure. I came back to the dorm for lunch, and I haven't seen him since."

"Maybe, it just seemed like someone was following you."

"No, Mom, it wasn't just like some other guy. He was clean-cut, short brown hair, older—like in his thirties—and good looking. And he looked intentional."

Her daughter sure had good observational skills. "Intentional?"

"Yeah, like he knew what he was doing."

Could this be the same guy who approached Josh on Friday? Two different campuses in three days. Kansas to Iowa—very doable, inside of one day. "Listen, Amanda, have you spoken with your father or Josh?"

"No, not yet. Should I?"

"No. I mean, not necessarily. Listen, I can tell you this much now…I have a situation related to my recent work teaching patients—"

"Is this some weird patient?"

"No, no. I've had a problem develop with the company I worked for. You don't need the details right now, but Josh was approached by someone last Friday at the Wheel in Lawrence." No matter what, she wasn't going to reveal the contents of Saturday's letter. Amanda did not have a need to know that. "An individual I'm working with on the situation arranged protection for you, me, and Josh just last night. So, you may notice someone hanging around."

God, it better be the protective detail.
"Protection? That sounds serious."

"I know it seems that way. Whatever. Listen, I have an idea. Why don't you snap a picture or two with your phone if you see him again? I can make sure it's someone with our security detail." Giving Amanda an assignment might help her feel useful. Might allay her fears. "What do you think, honey?"

"Sure, Mom. I'll try. If I see him again. But why do we need a security detail?"

"I'll explain soon, hon. And it may be a woman who's been assigned to you, so keep that in mind. And, Amanda, don't confide in your roommate or other friends. If you want to discuss this, please call me. It needs to stay inside a tight circle of involved people."

"Okay, Mom. But 'assigned to me'? What's going on? Are you okay?"

"I'm fine, and as this moves along, we'll be even finer. You take care and stay in touch. Keep a sharp eye out."

"Okay, I guess."

"Bye, honey."

"Bye, Mom."

Rachel waited only a few seconds before texting Carson. She had to confirm that Amanda's protection involved a thirtyish man, resembling Josh's Wheel guy. If not, then she'd jump in the car and speed off to Grinnell herself.

Running off pent-up tension took her around several additional blocks and off her usual course. She had let the detail know where she was going, and they'd unobtrusively followed along. At least she could think without worrying about being snatched along the way.

Carson hadn't called or returned her text. Damping down natural worry strained an effort. Of course, he'd returned home that morning, then said he'd be off to his office for the rest of the day. But this thing with the various characters now involved needed discussion. There was nothing to say, however, that even if this guy lurking around the Noyce building at Grinnell was one and the same as Josh's encounter, that another surveillance person couldn't keep an eye on him, too. Maybe it was all in place, everything covered. That realization helped propel her toward home with a small measure of relief. Running did clear her head. Most of the time.

As she neared her driveway, her cell chimed. She slowed to a fast walk and picked up. Finally, he…

"Hello?"

"Hi Rachel, this is Zera."

Oh. Not the person occupying her thoughts that day, but..."Hi, Zera, how're you?"

"Great!" Perpetually bubbly. "You sound like you're out of breath."

"Just finishing a run."

"Good, good. Well, I wanted to see how you were doing, and if you had any more questions about OAinvar."

"I guess I was waiting to hear if you had any more information about OAinvar."

"Information. Oh, you mean the side effects and the speed of approval."

"Yes, that's what I mean." Catching her breath, and cooling down, Rachel traced a circle around her driveway.

"I haven't been able to find out any more information about adverse reactions, yet. Nothing has come in our usual weekly email alerts from M-D," she whined. "And the person I need to speak to about the approval process is out of the office until Thursday."

Rachel said nothing. Zera hadn't called to tell her nothing. What was her real agenda? It didn't take too many more circles around her driveway to find out.

"Are you still there, Rachel?"

"Yes, I'm here."

"So, I heard a disturbing bit of news last Friday. But I didn't want to call you then."

"News?"

"Yes, I heard that you'd been let go from Advanced Education. What happened, Rachel? You were one of the best educators."

"Thanks for saying so, Zera. But that may be debatable. They apparently didn't like the way I completed their online forms, and two weeks ago today fired me." *Seems like two months ago*. "I thought you would have known before now."

"Oh, you know. So, what did you do that was so dreadful?"

"I filled out the column for adverse events, rather than calling it into the phone desk."

"No, really?"

"And that was against the rules, apparently."

"They didn't make that clear at the outset?"

"No. Not that I recall, and I don't think my memory has gone completely to pot. Not yet, anyway."

Zera paused, then asked, "It couldn't have been just you. Have you talked with any of the other educators?"

"No, no, I haven't."

"That's really terrible. Has anyone from the company called you back?"

"You mean AEC or M-D Pharma?"

"Well, either, really."

"Neither."

"I imagine you've discussed this with your family."

"No, not really."

"What do you think you're going to do?"

"Oh, I have some ideas, but no firm decision made yet."

"Care to share? I might be able to facilitate something."

Uh, huh, right. On guard, Rachel said, "Thanks, Zera, but I'm not going to make any sudden moves right now. I'd like to look over the landscape, study my options. You know."

"Sure. I understand. Have you heard, yet, who took over your territory?"

Is that the sound of my own teeth grinding? "Zera, how would I find that out?"

"I thought you might have heard."

"No. You'd be the one to tell me that, right?"

Ignoring her comment, Zera went on, "Oh say, I haven't heard any more about the lawsuit, either. But I'll keep digging around."

"Okay, sure."

"Listen, I've got to run. I'll be in touch." And the bubble machine hung up.

Rachel re-pocketed her phone, and headed into her garage, disgusted. Enough of Zera.

It was decision time: drive to Carson's office or pack a bag for a road trip to Grinnell College?

Twenty-Four

Thank goodness. Relieved, she scurried to the front hall. If he hadn't responded to her last text, she'd be halfway to Iowa by now, and no closer to an answer. She swung open the door, a bit too vigorously.

Carson gripped the storm door handle and admitted himself. "Sorry I took so long to answer. Was on the phone with two long-winded clients, and I needed to finish that. I knew the kids were safe, but I apologize for not communicating earlier."

She gave him a long look. "I guess you're forgiven. But I was about ready to take off on a fairly long drive."

He smiled and added a firm hug. "Oh, where to? You look great, by the way, since I saw you last at breakfast."

"Charm will get you everywhere." She returned his smile, disengaged, and walked to the kitchen. Serious then, she explained, "I was tempted to head to Iowa, to secure Amanda. I'm calmer than three hours ago, but still worried. Even though the protective detail is in place, what do you make of this guy Amanda noticed following her? Sounded a lot like the person who approached Josh in Lawrence last Friday."

"It does. And I share your concern. I relayed that to my friend. They're on it, he assures me. I should hear back by the end of the day." After a lull, he added, "Why don't we get something to eat and see what report we get after that?"

Two hours and one Friday's dinner later, they returned to

Rachel's. Just as she tended to her Krups machine, Carson's cell rang.

"Hey," he answered, clearly recognizing the caller. Listening for several minutes, he then said, "Okay. Right. So, we're on top of it? Sure. Keep in touch."

She should have asked him to put it on speaker.

When Carson ended the call, he turned to her. "It's what you thought. The Wheel guy is another player. Amanda's security detail is a very capable woman, ex-military, working with a male backup. And the guy she saw? Not sure it's the same guy who bugged Josh, but they're hunting for him."

Rachel nodded.

He went on, "Josh's detail is a man. They haven't seen anyone matching the description Josh gave of the Wheel guy still hanging around Lawrence. But that doesn't mean he fled and is in Grinnell."

"I know, but it makes me wonder. Maybe I should have Amanda come home for a couple of weeks." Rachel circled her kitchen island. "But, I don't want to disrupt her first semester."

"I don't think she should, Rachel. Of course, you can if you feel you must, but my friend is keeping us informed on a daily basis, more often if needed. He'll let us know if we need to change our tack."

"Does your friend have a name? And who decides if more often is needed?"

"He and I decide…okay, all three of us can decide if more frequent reports are required. And it's best you not know his identity for now."

She didn't much like the sound of that, especially where her kids were concerned, but she'd let it drop for the time being. Who cares what his name was, anyway? She said, "Amanda may snap a picture of anyone following her around. We can run that past your friend."

Carson nodded, "Sounds good."

Rachel let him know, "I received a call from my ex this morning. Apparently, Josh has been in touch with him about my 'situation' and his suspected tail. Nelson wasn't pleased, and he threatened to make things very uncomfortable if the kids are harmed. Of course, if the kids are harmed, he's the least of my concerns."

Carson took her in his arms. "I'll make sure nothing happens to your kids. Please trust me on this."

"It's hard, Carson. Hard."

"I know." He eased her away, and added, "Now, I've come with some other news. Good or bad, depends on how you take it."

"God, what now?"

"The contract…the forensic exam is done."

"Okay, so…?"

"That paragraph gives all the signs of having been inserted after the fact."

"How do they determine that sort of thing?"

"Hell if I know the specific techniques, but they're sure in this case."

"Unfortunately, I still can't find the original copy for comparison."

"That would seal it for sure, but I don't think you need it with this evidence."

"Did they put their opinion in writing or make a report?"

"In the works, as we speak."

She smiled. "That is such a relief. Wow. I am so grateful you suggested that." She paused, then added, "I may look further for my original. I never throw things like that away, and my habit is to make copies of everything I sign."

"Suit yourself, but with this evidence you don't need to endlessly search."

She made her way to the couch, sank down onto the cushions. Once Carson joined her, she said, "So, quite a Monday. And I haven't told you about my call from Zera Riordan, yet."

"No, you didn't. Interesting? Do I need a drink?"

"You might."

TWENTY-FIVE

Tuesday

Morning arrived none too soon. Rachel had spent the night up and down, tossing and turning, jarred from sleep too frequently by dream fragments involving children being chased by various animals or people, with her perpetually pursuing the whole mob. Of course, they never wound up anywhere specific. Nor did they fall off a cliff. It was not in the least restful. Twice, Carson had awakened when she'd sat up with a start. She appreciated his comforting, but knew it wouldn't solve this problem. Exhausted, he'd fallen soundly asleep around four a.m., not budging for the rest of the night.

Around six, with early light creeping around the drapery edges, Rachel abandoned her bed and made her way into the kitchen to brew coffee. Might as well start the day and close down the noxious night thoughts. At a reasonable time that morning she'd call the kids, just to reassure herself they could answer the phone. She picked up her mug and made her way into the family room. Twenty minutes later, she heard Carson's footsteps in the hall.

When he arrived, he paused to study her. "Did you get any sleep at all?"

"Yes, bits here and there. It's not like I've never lost sleep before. It'll be okay."

He plopped down on the couch next to her, laid his head on a back cushion, and took her free hand. "I know this is hard. Worse at night. But it's a new week, time to adjust our strategies. Maybe catalyze things to move in your direction."

"I agree. Enough of this nonsense. So, what's your recommended catalyst?"

"You remember what we discussed at dinner Saturday evening?"

"We talked about several things. You mean call the senator?" *How terrifying…*

"Exactly. Agitate things, move some of the chess pieces around." Getting up, he asked, "Any coffee left?"

Rachel sat at her desk, procrastinating. Carson was busy at the kitchen table taking care of business and checking in with his former FBI friend. He'd shooed her off to her office, giving her the privacy to make the call unobserved.

Having found the phone number on the internet, she stared at the list of legislators. She didn't make a practice of calling politicians' offices, whether local or national, and didn't much relish the prospect of putting herself out there. But, she reminded herself, she would undoubtedly speak with only a low-level staffer and then wait, perhaps days, for any kind of answer. *What's so scary about that? Nothing.* She picked up the phone.

After three rings, a melodious southern-accented voice answered, saying, "Senator Stanwood's office. How may I assist you?"

"Hello, my name's Rachel Quinn. I'm a nurse in Kansas City, calling with a concern about the FDA approval of a new drug." Not quite the whole truth, but hopefully it would suffice to get her through the screening process.

After a brief pause, the woman said, "Certainly. Why don't you give me your message? I'll forward it to the staffer who assists the senator with those issues, and he'll get back to you." Surprising. No, 'Why are you calling our office?' No, 'And why do you think the senator would be interested in that?'

Rachel gave the woman the information, and ended with, "Judith Grayson from the FDA called me just last week about this issue, and I'm expecting to hear back from her this week. My senator Mike Taggart also suggested I contact your office."

There was a long pause on the other end. Was she taking notes, or considering Rachel's name dropping? Finally, she spoke. "Senator Taggart referred you to our office?"

"Indirectly, through a friend with whom I'm working. Also, Judith Grayson mentioned the senator's name in conjunction with the FDA's efforts on the medication."

"All right. I think I have enough information to pass along to my associate and Senator Stanwood. Please give me your name again, and would you spell it? And your phone number and email?"

Rachel obliged.

The staffer then asked, "Would you mind giving me the name of your friend who knows Senator Taggart?"

Hesitating only a moment, she gave the young lady Carson's basic information. *He said he was overdue for some excitement, didn't he?*

"Thank you. We'll be back in touch."

"Thank you." They disconnected.

Rachel sat back, relieved, and considered whether she should be very hopeful based on such a conversation. It would be interesting to see how long before she received a response. Or, if she received one at all. Had she just made a move on the chess board? Queen to rook? Maybe they'd all sit and stare at the various pieces for a while. She checked her emails, deleted the lion's share, and left her office to update Carson. Time to hear the morning security report.

Carson looked up when she entered the kitchen and took a seat at the table.

"Did you reach them?"

"Yes, I did."

"And?"

"Well, I gave the senator's receptionist the basics, name dropped when it came to Judith Grayson and Senator Taggart, which seemed to get her attention. And I had to give her your name and number, too, as the contact person connecting me to Senator Taggart. She asked for it. It went fine. Not much more exchanged than that. Now we'll see how long it takes to get an answer from someone."

"May not be long."

"Do you know something I don't?"

He smiled.

"Don't tease me…are you on the inside loop?"

"No. No, I'm not. There are so many loops in Washington, how would you know which one qualifies as the inside orbit?" He finished his coffee, then added, "Want to hear the latest from security?"

"Absolutely."

Carson proceeded to relate the information his friend had compiled since last evening. Rachel was relieved to hear there had been no more sightings of the Wheel man identified by both Josh and Amanda. No other activity surrounding the kids had been observed. Things appeared quiet on both fronts. Carson and his former FBI friend, whom she had dubbed 'F^3', had agreed on twice daily briefings, unless something else occurred. The report from their own end had proved benign as well. It seemed black Range Rovers had effectively disappeared from the streets, or none had been noted cruising around in Rachel's vicinity. A day or two of quiet would be good.

But quiet could be unnerving, too.

TWENTY-SIX

It didn't take long for someone to stir the pot again. Sitting in Carson's office after lunch, gazing through the impressive window wall, Rachel waited.

He had relayed her contract to his legal department twelve days ago, to examine and render an opinion regarding the inserted paragraph. Any minute he would return with an attorney and sit down to make recommendations, if there were any to make. Her cell chimed—Josh. Apparently, he was not in class early that afternoon.

She picked up. "Hi, Josh."

"Hey, Mom. This a good time?" He sounded calm.

"Yes, it is. What's going on?"

"I should be asking you that."

"Well, you'll be glad to know I'm waiting at an office to receive a legal opinion about the clause in my employment contract, the one I mentioned Sunday when we spoke."

"Good. Anything else happening?"

"I heard from your father. I understand you spoke with him Sunday after our conversation."

"Yeah, I called Dad. He cares what happens, Mom. That's all. I thought he should know that things were going on."

"Of course, he cares what happens to you both, but my situation is none of his business, Josh. And I'm not consulting him about it."

"Okay, Mom."

"Any more sightings of the man who approached you Friday at the Wheel?"

"No, not him."

Just then, Carson and a forties-something female attorney strode through his office door. Rachel glanced up as they entered.

Relieved of the need to tell him about his surveillance team right then, she said, "Josh, I need to go. My counsel has returned with a verdict. May I call you tonight?"

"Sure, if it's before seven or after twelve. Got a study group between then."

"I pick the 'before-seven' slot. Talk with you then." Rachel hung up.

"Are we interrupting?" Carson asked.

"No, just finished. Josh."

He nodded. "Rachel, this is Margo Hamm, a member of our legal team. She'll give us her opinion about your contract, and the paragraph in question."

Margo stepped forward. "Hello, Rachel, good to meet you."

"Margo…"

"Would either of you ladies like some coffee?" Carson asked.

Both declined, more interested in discussion than decaf. "This shouldn't take too long," Margo said.

Carson and Rachel sat next to each other on the small settee. Margo Hamm took an adjacent club chair. She leaned toward Rachel as she spoke, exhibiting the contract to her, its text and margins now defaced with red ink.

"This is fairly straightforward. The usual language in the opening paragraphs outlining the legal employment relationship between the company and you. Nothing surprising there. When we get down to the bottom of page three, however, the change in font character and size raised concerns. I understand the forensic document people found evidence this was inserted later than the original contract preparation, likely after you submitted your signed copy and before they returned the finished copy to you."

"Yes, that's my understanding," Rachel confirmed.

Margo smiled and nodded. "The final page bears your dated signature and theirs as we would expect."

Rachel nodded. "Yes, that's my signature and the correct

date."

"So, back to page three. That later insertion violates contract law. We're left with what remedy you may have regarding your employment termination with this evidence that they essentially falsified the record, after the fact. I should ask you, before we proceed, what you want to see happen? Do you want to appeal your termination, given this information?"

"After all that's happened, I don't believe I want to appeal the termination. I'm not sure the harassment would stop, and frankly don't feel I want to associate with such an organization going forward."

"True. You have a point." Margo flipped the signature page over, and laid the document on the small table in front of them. Carson glanced at it. Margo said, "It sounds like there is more to the situation than I've been made aware of. What exactly do you mean by harassment?"

Rachel shot Carson a look. How many players were they going to mobilize? Would Mr. 'F-cubed' want this legal eagle weighing in on their activities, too?

He said, "It's up to you, Rachel, if you disclose what's happened."

Margo inserted, "You don't need to tell me everything but, as you're aware, I can give you a more thorough opinion if I know what you're up against."

"I think full disclosure is the best policy here," Rachel said. "I'd appreciate your complete opinion. It may direct my next moves."

She leaned back, crossed her legs, and launched into the brief, but convoluted history of the saga. Not forgetting her suspicions of Zera Riordan, she included summaries of those conversations and her impressions, but emphasized Advanced Education's comments and actions, and the harassment and tailing of her grown children and herself. Wearing a concerned expression, Margo glanced at Carson for confirmation, which he provided. Finishing with Judith Grayson's involvement and her call to Senator Jack Stanwood's office, Rachel paused.

Margo, making notes on her handy legal pad, remained quiet, clearly considering all that Rachel had relayed to her. Circumspect, she weighed in.

"Rachel, this has mushroomed into more than a grievance over an employment termination and a tainted contract, though that is sufficiently wrong to justify you bringing action. You did, by definition, sustain harm. However, this has bled over into the area of potential criminal activity. Then add political involvement to the mix. Have either of you reported any of this to the police?"

"No, we haven't," Carson answered.

"And your reason for not doing so?"

"Neither of us were sure it would amount to much."

Addressing Carson, she said, "You said you arranged for security surveillance for both of you, and for Rachel's children."

"Yes, but that's with a private firm I've used in the past for corporate security issues. The gentleman who runs it is former FBI."

Margo's brows shot up; her equanimous expression evaporated. "Okay, look, I suggest you get the authorities involved, other than a senator and an FDA panel member. They can't provide you with any ready protection. At least, I wouldn't count on that. I'm not disparaging your FBI friend, Carson. Just saying. Somebody here has too much to lose, and I think you all know which party that is."

"Definitely. And I share all of your concerns, Margo. We're likely not going to pull in the local authorities right now, but we appreciate your work on this," Carson said.

Rachel shot him a look.

Margo paused, regarded both, and said, "Okay, that's your decision, of course. Is there anything else I can do right now?"

"No. I think we're clear on your position. We need to discuss this, and we'll let you know if we have other questions." Carson stood.

Margo rose. "Very well. Good to meet you, Rachel. I'll let myself out." She strode toward the office door, saying, "Keep me posted," and she was gone.

Carson resumed his seat. He and Rachel sat silent for several minutes.

She broke the silence. "I'm not a bit surprised at her advice. And, basically, I agree with it."

"What's next?" he asked.

Rachel's cell chimed. She glanced at the screen and held it

toward him for his inspection.

"Not this," she said, swiping downward to dismiss Nelson's call.

~ ~ ~ ~

The doorbell rang. *Who could that be?* She put down her coffee mug and walked into the front hall. It wouldn't be Carson. She'd already given him a spare key. It seemed silly to make him stand on the front porch every time he came over, which was daily.

The bell rang two more times in rapid succession. *Impatient, aren't they?* She checked the peep hole, and saw the fish-eye figure of a uniformed young man standing there, staring at the door, his delivery van at the curb.

She opened the door and greeted him, "Hello."

"Rachel Quinn?"

"Yes."

"Package for you. Sign here," he added, extending an electronic pad toward her. She noticed the brown box tucked under his arm, a small cube bearing a label affixed to one side.

"I'm not expecting a package that I know of." She glanced beyond him to the delivery truck, and waited. It bore the name of a private delivery service she didn't recognize.

"Well, there's this one, for this address." He thrust the package at her.

"Okay, sure." She scribbled her name in the appropriate spot on his tablet. Handing it back to him, she accepted the package in return. *Very light weight.*

She watched him beat a hasty retreat to the curb, then returned indoors.

Examining the label as she walked to the kitchen, she picked up her reading glasses to take a closer look. The smudged return address and postmark made it impossible to recognize the sender. Whatever it was, it sure didn't weigh much. She pulled her zippo from a drawer and slit the tape securing the edges.

Opening the lid, and pushing aside a small layer of bubble wrap, she stared at the contents.

Absolutely nothing.

Twenty-Seven

Wednesday

The morning dawned cloudy; a dark ceiling hung low. It seemed the sky might open any minute and release a deluge of rain. Alone for a few hours, Rachel's mood matched the forecast. Impatient, she checked her emails every hour, hoping for a message from Judith Grayson. One week had passed since hearing from her. The Senator's office—no way they'd be back in touch so soon. Something, almost anything, needed to shift, needed to happen.

To say that she and Carson had obsessed the previous evening over the empty package would be an understatement. By the time he'd returned before dinner, she had already entertained numerous notions about its origin and possible microscopic contents. She'd donned medical exam gloves and moved the blank box to her garage, covering it with a handy trash bag for good measure. Not sure anything she'd use could adequately contain trace residue, nevertheless, she felt compelled to make an effort.

This was not some casual mistake of packaging, sent in error to her address. Had they missed a speck of powdered Anthrax, or some other horrid substance? Several times during the evening, they pulled out Rachel's magnifying glass and attempted to ascertain any granule or particle they might have overlooked. Wearing not only gloves then but, of course, surgical masks she had in her medical supplies. They'd consulted the internet. Maybe if they held it in better light…

They considered the wisdom of submitting it to the authorities, or at least F^3, for inspection. But then she, and probably Carson, would be required to go into isolation until the final answer came in. That seemed ridiculous and such an overreaction. And it might leak to the local media…*Woman Opens Empty Box, Suspects Domestic Terrorism*. No, they decided, they would not go that far. For the time being. So, they left it in the garage for the duration of the night, gingerly closing the lid, repeatedly scrubbing their hands and arms, and contemplated the situation. Both wondered whether they should sleep together that night. Would they be wafting something all over each other like *Pig Pen* emitting his impressive cloud of scum?

In the midst of all that, Rachel had returned Josh's earlier call, as agreed, before seven. Their spirited discussion did not, however, include any reference to the package situation. Thankfully, he'd truncated the call in time to make it to his study group. That cut short his haranguing her about dangers, legal recourse, his father's opinion, and other issues too numerous to count. To rein in his attitude, at one point, she disclosed their need for protective detail, at least in the near term, which silenced her aspiring lawyer son for a few moments. He then shifted his concern to Amanda's safety. How had Rachel caused all this? This just didn't make sense. Etcetera, etcetera.

She then diverted him with mention of the FDA panel member, and her contact with Senator Stanwood's office. Finally agreeing that perhaps she knew what she was doing, and that he'd try to be patient and give her some time to work it out, he circled back around to her new friend. Knowing full well Josh would tell his father, she finessed her answer, explaining that her friend's identity wasn't at the heart of the matter, and they could discuss that another time, soon. No way would she allow Nelson to undertake an investigation of Carson, which she had successfully deflected three years ago. Josh finally relented, ending the call.

But the night was still young when Nelson Quinn himself had shown up. No more concealing Carson. Having already enjoyed too much bourbon, Nelson laid on her doorbell a few too many times. Considering the strange package, and not expecting a respectable visitor at that hour, Carson answered the door. To say

Nelson looked shocked was an understatement. The two men engaged in a stare down for a few moments, then Nelson unleased a tirade which Rachel could recall clearly, although more than twelve uneasy hours had passed since then, during which she had enjoyed only a few hours of decent sleep.

Breaking the ice, Nelson had demanded, "What the hell? Who are you?"

"The name's Graham."

"What're you doing here?"

"That is frankly none of your business."

"The hell it isn't," roared Nelson. He attempted to pry the storm door from Carson's firm grip, as he maintained his position between Rachel and her rowdy ex.

She recalled Nelson pausing then and directing his attention to her, leaning around Carson and leering. "And you, dearie…don't you ignore my calls again, you hear?"

Wisely, she had refrained from answering his ridiculous, childish chastisement, and also restrained a laugh which threatened to erupt.

Without missing a beat, Carson intervened. "You need to leave before things get out of hand."

"Damned if you think you can order me around!"

And so on.

Finally, Carson had negotiated Nelson away from the door, and successfully propelled him to his Mercedes, parked not twenty feet from the porch. It surprised Rachel that her ex hadn't taken a swing at the man in the process, so revved up was he. One thing Carson failed to achieve, despite taking Nelson's keys away, was to convince him of his need for a ride home, even offering to haul her ex himself. But Nelson wrestled free of Carson's grasp and plunged into the driver's seat—while spouting more than a few colorful expletives—and arrogantly brandished an extra set of keys. Before Carson could wrest those away, and barely jump free of the car, Nelson executed a wild turn in her drive and sped off into the night to whatever fate. A smidgeon of concern and guilt still pestered her, but her conclusion overall…good riddance!

What a scene. It had taken more than an hour to settle down after that confrontation, and both agreed they felt spent by the time nine o'clock rolled around. Fed up, they finally settled on consulting 'F^3' in the morning. They retired irritated and troubled.

Mulling over the previous night, she retreated to the lower level and her weights. Maybe if she gave that a go, she'd pull herself out of the doldrums. She flipped on a favorite channel to stimulate distraction while she worked out. Finishing her upper extremities, she commenced her lower extremity work. Lunging with vigor, she barely heard her cell chime with a call. She sprang for the phone, expecting perhaps Carson on the other end with the morning security report. Surprised to see the Washington, D.C. area code, she paused before answering. Judith from the FDA, or Senator Stanwood?

Somewhat breathless, she managed a, "Good morning," and "Rachel Quinn here."

"Ms. Quinn, this is Senator Jack Stanwood's office." A more efficient woman's voice made the announcement. Rachel's stomach clenched. "You called yesterday about a certain matter involving the FDA."

My God, they're fast. "Yes, that's right."

"I'm going to transfer you to Senator Stanwood's aide, who handles those particular issues. Please hold."

Before Rachel could muster a response, canned classical music entertained her ear. She opted for pacing in the interim, gathering her thoughts as she circled. She chose not to run up the stairs to her office where her documents waited. She could arrange for an additional call with the aide if necessary. Perhaps, they were going to tell her to just bug off, it wasn't their concern, in diplomatic political-speak, of course.

She heard a click then another voice, this one male, came on the line.

"Ms. Quinn, this is Mark Keller, Senator Stanwood's aide. How are you today?"

"Fine."

"Good. I received your information yesterday and had the opportunity to discuss this with the senator. Yours is an intriguing inquiry which piqued his interest. You mentioned Judith Grayson, I believe, when you called. This is an issue he's worked on previously with the FDA. He is well acquainted with Ms. Grayson and respects her opinion very much. And Senator Mike Taggart is a good friend of his."

Rachel stopped pacing, and took the nearest chair.

"After sharing this with Senator Stanwood, he requested I call you back right away. One moment, please."

Rachel heard muffled sounds in the background, then Mark came back on the line. "Ms. Quinn, please hold for Senator Stanwood."

T*WENTY*-E*IGHT*

Thursday

Zera rose from the bed, grabbed his shirt, wrapped it around her, and padded into the large bathroom.

"I'm disappointed," he announced.

"I'm sorry, but I couldn't get more from her about who she's talked to." She shut the door, and shut out Parker, who lay in all his glory on the king-size bed. He wasn't pleased, and that worried her. Maybe she could just make up something. Enough to satisfy him. She turned on the shower.

He'd returned to town the previous afternoon under the pretense of needing another meeting with his regional sales force. Apparently, the higher ups in Charlotte weren't paying attention, or hadn't questioned his strategy for a 'required' workshop in Kansas City just eight days after his quarterly sales meeting. Parker had, no doubt, charmed them with his aggressive attitude and they'd given him free rein. She wasn't sure she should have. He planned to return home tomorrow, and she'd have the whole weekend to consider what she wanted. She had to come up with something about Rachel or kiss Dallas goodbye.

He'd chosen the Raphael for their tryst, the place he preferred on the Plaza whenever he made his own arrangements for travel to Kansas City, though that had been infrequent until recently. Zera had agreed, sure that if they were sighted by any of her friends no one would recognize or know Parker. And assuredly, they'd all wonder where Zera had found such a gorgeous man. No, they weren't likely to bump into any of her associates from M-D either, especially not for the two nights he'd be there. That was a safe bet.

Her shower finished, she returned to the room, a towel wrapped around her. Parker reached out as she passed, and caught her arm, reeling her in toward the bed.

"Come here." He attempted to strip the towel off, but she pulled away.

"Not now. I'm ready to do other things."

"What other things?" he asked, pushing up and propping himself against the pillows.

"Well, brunch for one thing. Then maybe some shopping."

"Shopping?"

"Yeah, I took the day off. The office isn't expecting me."

"I can't go by there, anyway. You don't have any sales calls to make?"

"No. Got all that done before you came."

"All right, let's see what we can come up with, then, for today."

He swung his legs over the side of the bed, and made his way into the bathroom. Good. She'd have time to dry her hair and dress if she hurried.

~ ~ ~ ~

He gazed at her through the coffee steam wafting from his cup.

They'd taken a small table in a back corner of the Classic Cup on the Plaza, the breakfast crowd exited and the lunch bunch not yet arrived.

"I know you want me to find out more. I've tried, Parker, but she's smart and stubborn. It's not easy to squeeze information from her."

"There must be some way."

"You'd think so. When I asked if she had talked to family, she said no, which I don't believe. When I asked if she'd tried to reach any of the other educators, she said no. Asked if she knew who had taken over her territory, she in turn asked how would she know about that? She put it back on me. You know, 'Zera, how would I find that out?' When I asked her what she planned to do, she said she had some ideas. She used the phrase, 'look over the landscape, study my options.' Said she was not making any moves right away."

"What do you think she means by 'options'?"

"Hell, if I know. I asked her if she'd care to share. She declined."

"Maybe she has her guard up. Doesn't trust you."

"If so, it's not because I've done anything, ever, to create distrust."

He smiled. "Have you ever seen her with anyone?"

"You mean like a man?"

"Precisely."

"She divorced, I think, three or four years ago."

"Oh? You know anything about her ex?"

"Not really. I think she once said that he's a lawyer."

"Did she ever mention a firm?"

Parker seemed a little too interested, in her estimation. Better to avoid any further talk of Rachel's former marriage. He might just give her another assignment. Or, poke around where he shouldn't. It wouldn't be good to tangle with a lawyer ex-husband.

"Not that I remember. And she's never mentioned seeing anyone recently, and I haven't seen her around with a man."

"Might be worth checking into."

"Short of spying on her, how would we do that?"

"Exactly." He smiled and took another sip of steaming coffee. "This frittata is sure good."

~ ~ ~ ~

She felt like she was in high school, cruising by a boy's house with her girlfriends. How utterly embarrassing. This time, if things got tense, she could shrink down or go to the floor. Get out of sight.

They had found Rachel's address on the AEC website, which Zera could access for all of the area instructors. Easy as pie. Maybe that had scored some points with Parker. Participating in a drive-by should also rack up some serious equity. Hoping so, she could see Dallas coming into focus, a bit clearer now.

Midafternoon, and the subdivision gate stood wide open as usual. The brick wall enclosing the entire neighborhood established the owners' territory, discouraging would-be intruders. A cozy development, there were only three blocks to cover. Researching before they had embarked, they'd noted two homes on the market, a nice ruse for their casual drive-through.

They turned in.

Glancing from side to side as they crawled along, she took in the architecture, size of the homes—some dual homes, some single units—the privacy fences, landscaping, and the presence of barking dogs or not. French country designs, some with entrance courtyards, created an air of elegant charm. Zera found herself distracted by the atmosphere, desiring to look at the few houses on the market more than surveille Rachel and whomever. The streets were quiet that Thursday, only one car passed by throughout their course.

Before they realized they were close, they saw the address painted on the driveway curb and slowed. Surprised to see a dark blue Lexus sedan parked in the drive, they shared a look. Someone *was* there. When Parker questioned her earlier, Zera thought Rachel drove a Honda, at least from past conversations she could recall. They continued past the next two homes, parked at the curb in front of a home sporting a *For Sale* sign, and pretended to study a listing sheet.

Not ten minutes later, Zera glanced in her side mirror. She noted a man emerge from Rachel's garage. He went to the car, bent inside in an obvious search for something, then stood in the vehicle's open door. The garage door gaped open, a Honda Accord sat parked inside. She reached over and grabbed Parker's arm as the garage door slid down.

"There is someone. A man, at the Lexus."

Parker strained to look over his right shoulder. "Have you ever seen him before?"

"No, never. She has a son, but he's young, in his twenties."

"That guy's older, probably fifties."

"Right. Oops…there she is, coming out the front door. We need to get out of here." Zera slid down in her seat.

"She can't see you or recognize you from the back of your head. Don't worry."

"Well, we've sat here long enough to decide if we're interested in seeing this house. I don't want her neighbors to report a strange car camped out at their curb."

"Relax."

Oh, right. Far from it. "I don't make a habit of going on stakeouts." She went on, "They're leaving, and coming this way. Shit."

"Okay, calm down. We'll cruise down the block, and park in front of the other place that's on the market. That'll keep anyone from wondering."

"Better get moving…now."

~ ~ ~ ~

"You really don't need to go with me on these errands."

"I know, but with everything going on, it's best I do."

"Oh, look, there's someone interested in the Anderson's place," Rachel said, as they drove past the new charcoal grey Ford Explorer parked at the curb. "Looks like a young couple…Wait!"

"What?"

"I could swear that was Zera Riordan, the drug rep, sitting in the front seat of that car with a guy."

"You've got good eyes." Carson craned his neck to catch a glimpse, but couldn't manage a decent view in the seconds before the road curved away. "Want to circle back around?"

"I'd feel stupid being so obvious. Then what would I do, wave? Or stop and say how surprised I am to see her there. Besides, it's probably not her. She's not married, and I'm not aware she has a steady man. If it's her, why would she be looking at houses in this neighborhood? It's not a place young couples seek out."

"Precisely."

Rachel glanced at Carson. "Do you think?"

"Hell if I know. If you're pretty sure, then what is she doing here hanging out with some man in broad daylight?"

"True. Suit yourself, then."

"I'll circle back around. We can even go back to the house, and you can pretend to get something you forgot from the garage."

Giving his idea a moment's thought, she nodded. "Let's go."

Taking a right turn, away from the entry gate, circling around the next street and ultimately curving back onto Rachel's street, they undertook the ruse of the forgotten item left at home. Once accomplished, they made their way again around the bend toward the entrance.

The 'for sale' house sat vacant, no cars nor interested parties anywhere in sight. No realtor waiting in an open door, apparently stood up by capricious buyers.

Not coincidental, definitely suspicious, and absolutely concerning.

TWENTY-NINE

Sunday

The ride proved bumpy from time to time. Enough turbulence to be annoying and, as a result, the seatbelt sign remained on. Skilled at their balancing act, however, the flight attendants continued cabin service. The first-class seats were certainly an added pleasure. She'd considered asking for strong drink, but limited herself to one glass of wine and after that, only club soda garnished with a lime. The two-and-a-half-hour flight allowed for welcome thinking time, and she needed to keep a clear head.

The remainder of the previous week had proved quiet, except for preparation for this trip. And the examination of the empty package she'd received Tuesday which they'd referred to Carson's former FBI friend. He'd completed that evaluation at an undisclosed lab by late Friday. As expected, nada, nothing. Thank goodness they'd not rung all the area alarm bells. So, other than that little blip in the road, only laundry, paperwork, another conversation with Judith Grayson, the post office and other errands—always with an eye on the rear-view mirror—had consumed their time. And making sure her children were safe, with protection in place, before she took off on the next leg of this adventure.

It seemed like a month since last Sunday when Josh had called about the strange guy in Lawrence, when Amanda had 'disappeared', and Carson had come to occupy her bed. She glanced out the plane's window. Flying east, she admired the coral-tinged clouds and deepening blue sky, remnants of a fading sunset receding behind her.

The month was at its end. October first would arrive Tuesday. The one September day remaining, filled with what? It was hard to predict, and she was very tired of trying to project what might happen next. Incredible, all that had occurred in three short—or long—weeks since Saturday, September seventh. Since Linda Bates lay writhing on her bathroom floor. Usually in control of her circumstances, she had never before found herself in such a situation.

What exactly was this situation? A position ending abruptly, orchestrated not by her, but another party? Someone tailing her, a strange empty package, harassment directed at her children? Entangling herself in a speedy relationship with a man? Granted, she'd known him a good while, but allowing things to move at warp speed? When it's right, sometimes you don't need months to figure it out. You just move ahead. But not her, not any of this, at least never before. Had she really led such a sheltered life? It certainly didn't feel that way, looking back.

Now, what was she doing…posing the questions, and taking only her own counsel?

She glanced at the occupant of the adjoining seat. He had dozed off shortly after the beverage service. Leaning back against the headrest, she closed her eyes, too. Time to shut down her disquieting thoughts. There would be hours enough for that during the coming week. The engines' hum muffled other passengers' quiet conversations. With everyone around her appearing unruffled, she pretended to relax.

Carson reached over and took her hand, delivering a light squeeze. It seemed he had registered her thoughts, after all.

Thirty

Monday

Rachel followed the young man down the tiled corridor. The sterile-appearing pale green walls reminded her of the older hospitals where she'd spent many hours, working or teaching. Office doors to this side or that could have been patients' rooms in her former world. Various pictures interrupted the bland walls, benign landscapes which rarely inspired gazing. Midway, they turned into a stairwell, climbing a short flight to the floor above and a more welcoming reception area.

The green walls morphed to a warm grey taupe. Obviously, recent renovations had transformed this area. Apparently, the federally-contracted remodelers hadn't yet made it to the ground floor. Old commercial carpet gave way to faux wood floors with carpet inserts at strategic gathering spots. Gone were the harsh fluorescents, replaced by more pleasing recessed lighting. New contemporary furnishings provided comfortable seating, and several faux plants softened the institutional landscape. The young man indicated she should take a seat, then hurried off toward the end of the hall, to disappear around the corner. Rachel picked up a recent magazine, and waited.

She felt a pair of eyes resting on her and glanced up. A young female receptionist wearing ear buds stared at her over the edge of the elevated counter. Only the upper portion of her face was visible. Rachel wasn't sure if she was enjoying her favorite tunes, or listening to a dictated document, or assessing her. Her smile elicited one in return from the young woman, though Rachel could only see her eyes crinkle in response.

The receptionist asked, "Would you like a bottled water?"

"No, thank you, I'm fine." Better to avoid too many additional bathroom breaks.

Acknowledging with a nod, the receptionist returned to whatever work was set before her.

To pass the time, Rachel took out her cell, scanned through emails and any texts she may have missed and deleted a few unneeded ones. Carson was out there somewhere, and she was anxious to know how he was progressing.

Soon, the young man materialized again. "Ms. Quinn, please come with me."

Rachel stood and followed him down the hall to its end. After a left turn, then a quick right, she found herself entering a small, windowless conference room. A woman waited there at an oval table. She stood.

"Hello, Rachel. I'm Judith Grayson." She smiled easily, extending her hand.

Not knowing what to expect, despite her Google search, Rachel had to admit she was a bit surprised.

"Please, take a seat."

A tall figure of a woman, the redheaded Judith resumed her seat before Rachel could choose one and sit. A snarl of long red curls encircled her head and, if sunlight had been permitted, would have created a halo effect. She wore scant makeup, but didn't require much. Her natural beauty was, at once, evident. She wore a stylish, conservative beige suit and light blue blouse, all of which served as a neutral backdrop. Rachel could see why people would notice, and remember, this person. She projected a professional, well-put-together image.

"Thank you."

"I appreciate you coming on short notice. I trust your trip went well."

"Yes, it did."

"Good." Judith broke eye contact and fiddled with her sleek laptop to her left. "I have the data you sent along last week, and have reviewed it. We'll take a look at that shortly. Do you have any questions for me before we begin?"

"No, not before we look at that."

"I should let you know, we're in this particular room because it is away from other offices, and is considered secure. No eyes, no ears. It's swept twice daily."

Reassuring? Perhaps not the need for such a space, though. Rachel nodded.

"Would you mind retracing for me the initial incident which seemed to precipitate this whole process?"

"Sure." Rachel succinctly related the Linda Bates teaching session, her alarm at the patient's reactions, and her recording of the details of the encounter. She explained the internet interruption, which prompted her to check with Advanced Education Concepts the following Monday regarding her submission of the patient report. And she detailed for Judith the ensuing three conversations with the two individuals at AEC, which led to her termination.

After a few clarification questions from Judith, Rachel proceeded to itemize the incidents of harassment directed at her and her children during the intervening several weeks. The FDA panelist paid particular notice to her account, drilling down on details of those events or encounters. Rachel concluded with the forensic document report and legal opinion from Carson's company, as well as her contact with Senator Stanwood's office.

When Rachel finished, Judith paused and collected herself. Under the guise of an inquiry, she proceeded to make statements and pose a few questions—about Carson's company, the timeliness of his sudden appearance on the scene, and his interventions on behalf of Rachel.

At once surprised and uncomfortable, Rachel wondered if they—the FDA—had sent Carson in on her case, or were they just glad he had appeared and could be of assistance? Her guard shot up. Now it was time for her to ask some questions.

Done with that, Judith angled her laptop toward Rachel and pulled up a screen for Mynard-Drexel Pharmaceuticals. Scrolling down through the FDA's front page on the company, she came to their list of medications, and tapped on the first in line. Not Arthremimab.

"We see data here on this one which has been on the market now for seven years. Given your situation, we checked back on their reporting data, and found some evidence of gaps." Hitting the back button, she returned to the main page. She hit the next drug's hyperlink, pulled up the following page, and went through the information on that drug which had enjoyed substantial market success over the past five years. According to Judith, the data there seemed in line.

Next came OAinvar—Arthremimab.

"Here we go. We have four years of post-market data on it, two years for its osteoporosis indication. As you and I suspected, the adverse event percentages are off, way too low. They didn't bear up under statistical scrutiny." She looked at Rachel.

"Ironically, using Advanced Education Concepts for their patient education only made our job easier. It's incredible that this oversight on their form—leaving that Adverse Events column in place—caused them to trip up. If they'd just eliminated that, and made clear to the instructors to call in AEs, we'd never have known they were messing with their data. Or, at least that's my opinion." She scooted the laptop away and leaned back, meeting Rachel's gaze.

"And, as we discussed in our first phone call, the approval process was expedited. I haven't made a big deal with the other panelists yet about that process two and a half years ago, but I did speak with several of them who had agreed with me at the time. They're concerned, too. We'll obviously have to address that issue again, very soon. In the meantime, we can opt to put out a warning on the med, after we notify the company of our concerns. They have a ninety-day remedy period they can pursue, if they so choose. In this case, I don't think they'll just yank it.

"I will say to you, two panelists who voted for Arthremimab's speedy approval are very uncomfortable with this situation. I surmised that when I recently touched base with them. Then when I probed further, they deflected. It's possible they may have enjoyed some benefit or quid pro quo for their original position. Naturally, we're looking into it." She paused briefly, then said, "This should remain quiet for now. You and I won't discuss it again until I signal that we can. I'm sure you understand."

Completely. "Yes, I do."

"So, questions?"

Rachel inquired about housekeeping details related to record retention, release or protection of her identity on the previously submitted FDA information form, and alluded to another app which she had secured elsewhere—her patient list, and that of other educators—which might reflect a HIPPA violation. Judith visibly alerted to that particular comment, indicating they would discuss that issue later, too.

Rachel then circled back around to Judith's specific questions regarding Carson. "I'm curious…" She paused, then asked, "Did you know of Carson Graham before he contacted me in early September?"

Judith sat back, gave her a long look, and said, "Let's take a break for now. We'll discuss those issues a bit later. Hungry?"

THIRTY-ONE

He wheeled around the corner with his foot just tapping the brake. The numerous traffic circles in D.C. hadn't sufficiently discouraged the large SUV following them. Or, at least the vehicle he thought was following them. Perhaps, they should pursue an alternate course, take off in a different direction. These guys were good, and they were going to have to do something more dramatic to shake them.

Carson glanced at his passenger. The woman riding shotgun was a dead ringer. He couldn't have picked a better look-alike. The woman, the vehicle, all of it supplied by a friend of a friend at the FBI. She was calm, even smiling at times, obviously more adept at this than him. And currently enjoying herself. He was certain she'd read his thoughts.

"Any ideas?" he asked.

"You're doing fine. Just keep to the left, then shoot off onto M Street when we complete the Penn Avenue NW circle again. Turn right four blocks from there at 33rd and go north. They should have some trouble keeping up. I suspect we'll lose them after that."

Carson followed orders, swerving at just the right moment, veering onto the straight away on M, running a yellow light at Wisconsin, hanging a right just as directed at 33rd Street, and disappearing into light commercial traffic in Georgetown. She didn't give more directions for the next ten minutes, as Carson took whichever streets he pleased, navigating the one-way maze.

"Any other instructions, or do I just turn here and there as I see fit?"

"We're going toward Wisconsin again. When we get to that intersection, hang a right and go south to N Street. Turn right there and go west to 33rd Street, where you'll turn right again. Take that north to P Street and turn left. Go west on P to 36th Street and turn left again. One block south is O Street, turn left there. Halfway down the block on the right is a narrow drive between buildings behind Holy Trinity School. Holy Trinity Catholic Church is right next to it. We'll pull into that narrow drive, ditch this car in their parking lot, and pick up another left there for us. I'll show you. That should buy us a bit of time."

Sounded like a plan. If he could remember all of it. Otherwise, he had none.

"Remind me again as we go. Or, why don't we switch and you drive?"

"No, you're fine."

Okay then.

Rachel had been picked up that morning by a special car sent to their hotel to fetch her. Whether the FDA provided the transportation, or the Senator's office, or even the FBI, it didn't matter. She was safely conveyed to her destination. Carson's assignment—the fun of running pursuers all over town with a double who could be Rachel's twin. The FBI were good. Where they found these people, he had no idea. She was either an agent, or perhaps an actress/model, and he hoped the former. She was beautiful and this was fun. Unless, of course, it deteriorated and got nasty. Then it would be good if both of them were armed and knew what to do. He was. He assumed she was, as well.

Fifteen minutes later, they accomplished the vehicle switch. She said, "When we come to the next light, turn right then take a quick left. Halfway down the block, you'll see an old brick warehouse on the left. There's a very short driveway to a single garage door…it will go up automatically when we approach. Drive straight in, park to the right side, and kill the engine. They're expecting us."

Yes, ma'am. "Right." His was not to question. At least there they'd have some reinforcements. Or whoever was 'expecting' them.

"You handle the car well. Done this before?"

"Can't say that I have."

Three hours later, and after lunch with the Rachel double and a group of men who happened to be federal agents, Carson wondered aloud when he'd see Rachel again.

"Later this afternoon, we'll pick her up at the FDA. From there you'll be driven to another venue for the night."

"Why a change in location?"

"Your hotel's been compromised."

That sounded problematic. "Compromised. What about our stuff?"

One very serious agent looked at him. "Yes. Compromised." The middle-age suited man offered no further explanation, but did add, "Your possessions have been secured."

Carson didn't press for more information. Probably one of those need-to-know things, and he was better off not knowing what the compromise entailed.

"There's a room in the back where you can wait. Make yourself comfortable."

Definitely not a suggestion. Carson turned and navigated his way toward the back of the small warehouse bay.

The whole set up resembled a tech business newly opened in Georgetown in a refurbished gentrified brick building. Except for the one suited agent, who resembled a harried CEO, various other individuals hung out in jeans and long-sleeved tee shirts or casual sweaters. Mostly men, and a few women—sporting long hair, short hair, green hair, purple hair, tattoos, or funky eyeglasses—populated the space. All of whom appeared more than fit. He was sure it was a tech company, just not the commercial enterprise you might expect if you happened in. He hoped there was good coffee waiting in the lounge, and maybe a TV to pass the time, though, in the middle of the day he had little idea of what he'd watch. Perhaps a nap was in order.

Entering the spacious room, he took in the space with one sweeping glance. A well-equipped galley kitchen graced the wall to his left. A new L-shaped sectional sofa occupied the opposite wall and protruded into the open seating area. Adjacent to that sat two leather recliners, a table between them. No litter or leftovers to be seen. These people were really neat. They probably incinerated all their uneaten food and flushed unwanted beverages.

Two tall narrow windows, representative of the building's beginnings in the late 1800's, pierced the wall straight ahead, their opaque glass allowing in only diffuse light. He suspected the glass was very new and very high tech. Retractable black shades hung in both, half-pulled. And in the adjacent corner hung a new, huge, digital TV. No doubt there were concealed cameras mounted at various positions. He'd ignore that thought for the present. This would be a very comfortable spot in which to relax. He turned toward the kitchen to scrounge for coffee. Undoubtedly, it would be a late night.

~ ~ ~ ~

They cut the corner and, five seconds later, turned into an underground parking garage. Two men wearing official looking attendants' uniforms stood near the open entrance, their chests enhanced and squared by concealed vests, their belts weighted with weaponry. Not at all persons you'd mess with. They waved them in, and the automatic garage door descended. They pulled to a stop in front of a plain, gray metal door. The agent riding shotgun jumped out, scanned the garage, moved to the door, and pressed an unlabeled gray button next to the door frame.

Carson watched from the middle seat of the blue Suburban. Besides the driver and shotgun passenger, another man occupied the third-row seat behind him. No one conversed until the door opened and there stood Rachel, looking quite composed in the company of a security guard.

"Okay, there she is," Carson said.

No one else spoke. He watched as the guard nodded to the agent, who took Rachel's arm and escorted her to the SUV. The grey metal door closed silently behind them. She was shown to the middle row seat beside Carson, and the van's door quickly slid shut.

"All right," the driver suggested, "let's get this show on the road." Shot-gun rider vaulted in.

They exchanged a look as Carson reached over and took her hand. "Good to see you."

She nodded, gave him a small smile, but said nothing.

The driver executed a quick turn, and wheeled the large SUV across the garage toward the automatic door. The door rose. The guards waved them through. Out into the open again.

Fifteen minutes later, and after what seemed a few diversionary tactics just for good measure, they turned a corner in Georgetown, where sat a beautiful vintage townhome, and pulled into a rear driveway. Carson noted a warm glow in the front and side windows as they rounded the corner. Again facing a single garage door, it rose and they drove in. Obviously, a new addition to the lot, the garage occupied half of the rear garden area. Built to blend in with the period architecture of the neighborhood, it resembled an established carriage house. The automatic door smoothly slid down behind them.

Once disembarked, they were directed to a side door which, when opened, revealed a set of stairs descending to what appeared to be a tunnel. What a set up. Carson and Rachel both hesitated for a moment. Is going down into a tunnel a good idea at that moment? Carson, for one, wasn't sure.

Exchanging a glance, and apparently deciding in unison to avoid a balk, they undertook the steep descent, one agent in the lead, two other agents bringing up the rear. Traversing the short passageway to the house, with delectable food smells beckoning, they climbed a set of stairs again and found themselves in a new kitchen, staring at a plump, red-faced cook efficiently tending pots and plates. Someone shut a door behind them.

"I hope you're hungry," she said with a smile. "Dinner's almost ready."

That was the best news he'd heard all day. Rachel broke into a broad smile. "Smells wonderful."

Despite the smile, she was obviously worn out. But he hoped she'd revive long enough, after what promised to be a memorable dinner, to fill him in on what had happened at the fortress. Unless, other more important activities intervened.

"This way," said one of the agents, gesturing toward a front room.

THIRTY-TWO

October 1st, 2019

Awakening to the smell of bacon was not a bad thing at all. The ruddy-faced cook must be at it again, Carson realized, as his eyes eased open. Though the room was still basically dark, early light crept through the shutter edges. October first. They would both likely remember this day for a long time. He turned to his right and appreciated the curve of her hip as she lay, facing away, beside him.

Not sure it was true about no spying equipment in the bedrooms, they'd opted anyway to occupy the same room, same bed, that night. But not give anyone anything to look at if monitors were inadvertently engaged. Frustrating yes, but they coped. While watching a good deal more late-night TV than desired, they carried on whispered conversations about their day, intently interested in each other's escapades. Rachel had seemed to him more reserved than usual, had brought up 'coincidences' with regard to his first phone call and subsequent pursuit, and expressed curiosity concerning his motives. He stayed calm, and thought he offered sufficient answers, but he wondered where her prodding might lead. Postponing any further analysis, they had both drifted off around one a.m.

Rachel stretched and turned to face him. She smiled.

"Good morning."

"Morning. Ready for the next adventure?"

"Guess so."

After a lingering hug, they parted and rose.

~ ~ ~ ~

The automatic doors slid open. They walked through, and immediately stopped. Security personnel and scanners stood guard. A short line had formed, all waiting to be processed. With their armed, plain-clothes escorts positioned in front of and behind them, they were expedited through.

Done with the security checkpoint, they hustled down a long hall to a bank of elevators. Riding swiftly upward, they stepped out onto the third floor. Signaled to move to their right they reached a corner, paused, then turned left. It was hard to ignore the fourteen-foot ceilings, well-worn terrazzo floors, and the ornate woodwork preserved from previous eras.

Carson would have preferred to linger and admire the handiwork, but they were hurried down the corridor, coming to a stop in front of an impressive door, a small brass sign to the left bearing the familiar name. He was being deposited there to presumably visit his old college buddy. If not for Rachel Quinn, perhaps there would have been no such visit. At least not then.

They said their goodbyes, and in he went. What they were going to talk about for hours, he had no idea. Maybe some new initiatives voters would favor? Old times, college sports, or the state of a beleaguered fraternity system? Most likely, though, they wouldn't have to fill nearly that much time.

~ ~ ~ ~

Rachel felt as if she was living someone else's life. What did she have to do with federal oversight, FDA approvals, or officials jockeying for higher positions? This was the first day of October. What on earth had happened to her since stepping foot in that darkened house on September seventh? Yikes.

She took a deep breath, squared her shoulders, and forged on with her two escorts, an aide on one side, an armed agent on the other. Who would have thought?

She wasn't exactly sure what she was going to say once inside the office, but she trusted appropriate words would come. After all, they had asked her to come. And considering her day with Judith Grayson, she expected her host would be well-versed. They arrived at an auspicious looking door. The aide smiled, opened the door and motioned her and her escort into the very small ante-room.

"Good morning," he greeted his associates. "This is Rachel Quinn, from Kansas City. And this is Agent Smith. He'll be waiting."

Introductions completed, Rachel took her appointed seat on an antique settee under a large painting of a battle waged centuries before somewhere in Virginia. The agent was efficiently shuffled into an adjoining office by the pert receptionist, who appeared anxious to make his acquaintance. Though offered coffee, Rachel declined, already feeling she might have to get up and pace if it was a lengthy wait. It was not.

Less than five minutes later, an adjacent door eased open, and a tall, patrician figure of a man filled the space. He smiled, looked down at Rachel, and opened the door wider.

"Ms. Quinn, please, do come in," he drawled.

THIRTY-THREE

"Do sit down."

Rachel chose one of two seats in front of his massive walnut desk and perched on the front edge. A display of good posture seemed prudent.

Senator Jack Stanwood retired to his desk chair, took up his reading glasses, and shuffled several piles of papers on his desk, clearing a spot onto which he placed a slim brown folder.

Is my name on the top tab?

"Do you care for a coffee or tea?"

"No, thank you."

He pressed a button on his intercom and instructed an aide to bring him a steaming, fresh cup of coffee, sugar, no cream. He then turned his attention to Rachel and paused before speaking.

Folding his hands on the file folder, he said, "I do appreciate you coming in today. Making time for these discussions."

"I appreciate your office inviting me and helping with the arrangements."

"We're glad to do it. Although, Judith's office did most of the legwork on that."

"Yes."

"So, Ms. Quinn, you have quite a story here. Now, you're aware that I know Ms. Grayson very well, and respect her and her work at FDA. We've collaborated a number of times on issues at the FDA, at hearings and such. She's a very capable, diligent woman."

"Yes, I believe I would agree."

His secretary entered, smiled at Rachel, and set the steaming cup of coffee on the senator's desk. She quietly retreated and silently closed the door behind her.

He took a careful sip. "She's brought me up to speed about your day yesterday, and the ins and outs of how your situation first developed. Really quite remarkable. Tell me, how did you come to work for the company…Advanced, what was it?"

"Advanced Education Concepts."

"Yes, yes, of course."

He should know that… "Apparently, I was recruited."

"Do you know by whom?"

Rachel paused. This was at the heart of the matter. She gave him her well-rehearsed response.

"I was looking for a different position about two years ago. I received what I thought was a generic email solicitation, and checked out their website. I researched them further, asked a few follow up questions, and someone there contacted me. We discussed, and I eventually agreed to give it a go."

The senator gazed at her as she spoke. He asked, "Did you ever meet the individual with whom you spoke, the one who contacted you?"

"No, I never met that person. Why?"

"I think you can appreciate why I'm asking, where this line of questioning may lead."

Rachel didn't answer, merely gazing back at Senator Stanwood. *Where was this leading?*

He smiled and leaned back in his well-worn leather chair. Growing serious then, he said, "So, here we are. One thing you may not be aware of, and I'm sure you've wondered about, is why I'm so interested in this whole deal."

He went on, "I've told you, and Ms. Grayson has as well, how we've worked together on FDA issues. Pretty par for the course. But, several years ago, we both became aware of flaws, shall we say, in the drug approval process. She questioned the bias of several of her colleagues on the approval panel. Further observation revealed the possibility that insiders were skewing data to ensure speedy approvals. But, how were they doing it? Who might they be working with or for? And what was in it for them? All difficult questions to answer. We didn't have specifics to hang our hats on. So, we launched our own discreet investigation, developed our own behind-the-scenes personnel, or team, you might say." He smiled.

It was crystallizing...she now understood her role. *I do declare.*

"And that's where individuals such as yourself come in."

Rachel felt some sort of comment, or question, was in order. "Senator Stanwood, are you saying I was a *plant*, unbeknownst to me?"

"Precisely. And you did a damn fine job of it." A broad grin spread across his face.

Rather than conveying shock, Rachel responded with a smile, as well.

"Matter of fact, your recruiter was someone we'd positioned there, at Advanced Education Concepts, to recruit individuals such as yourself...people of integrity, with unimpeachable credentials and employment histories. Smart people who could be trusted to do their job well. And notice things. Advanced Education wasn't the only company where we placed folks. At any rate, that effort is ongoing so, of course, this conversation stays here."

"Of course." She gathered her thoughts. "Senator, I do have a question."

"By all means."

"Who precisely is 'we'?"

"Why, the FDA and my office. Several others at necessary agencies. Actually, just me here, and Mark Keller. My other office staff don't know the specifics I've worked on with Judith. These walls have ears, you know, and one can never plug up all the damn leaks around here."

"Okay, so when I was 'placed'..."

"Identified, is a better choice of word."

"All right, identified. Did you all know of my eventual firing?"

"No. We did not. But we developed several scenarios in advance, so we could prepare for how to deal with you, and others, if various situations, that being one, arose."

Deal with me? "I see."

"We basically knew what we were going to do if that transpired. And, if you became the target of any harassment."

"So, Carson Graham?"

Stanwood smiled, "He became convenient."

"Through his acquaintance with our Senator Taggart?"

"I'll not say at this time."

"Am I to take it that, he, an acquaintance of mine, arrived on the scene at just the right time, to render assistance to me following development of this particular situation at Advanced Education Concepts, which you did not orchestrate, and which may have caught you and Judith Grayson by surprise?"

"I'll not say at this time."

"Respectfully, sir, that's all just a little hard to believe."

"Perhaps so, but let's just let that rest for now. Here's another thing, and this may not be so hard to believe. Shortly after you filed that patient's report with AEC, and you were reprimanded and then fired, I received an offer of a sizable campaign contribution from M-D Pharma. Now, it's not unusual for industry officials or even private companies to offer such, but the size of the contribution and the timing was just too coincidental. So, we knew you'd uncovered something. We shifted gears and began watching your arena. And began to dig around further."

"Amazing."

"Yes. And so you'll know, you and your family were never in danger. We had people all over the place."

There certainly were people all over the place. "That's good to hear. Not that it's my business, but I am curious. What happened with M-D Pharma's campaign offer?"

"Flat turned it down. And, of course, they're being investigated for campaign finance violations by the FEC."

"It's unfortunate they attempted that. The company has several successful medications. Judith showed me the FDA's information and the statistical reports. I hope they're not pulled from the market."

"We'll have to see. She brought me up to speed, as well, before you arrived."

His aide Mark stuck his head in the door about that time, letting the Senator know of a committee meeting in fifteen minutes.

The senator turned back to Rachel. "Bottom line, as this case is lateralled to those who'll pursue it, we'd like you to consider something."

Rachel's stomach clenched, churning her breakfast bacon.

"We believe it's advantageous to have people such as yourself in positions within the pharmaceutical industry. Various positions, and not just teaching, to surveille situations we think are suspicious or questionable. We'd like you to consider accepting a position on an ongoing basis."

Shocked, Rachel sat speechless. If she wasn't mistaken, this senator had just offered her a job of industry spying. *What a twist.* "I'm not sure what I think of that. This is…unexpected."

"Well, think about it, Rachel. Judith will stay in close contact with you. We hope you give our offer thoughtful consideration." He paused, then said, "Of course, you may be called as a witness in any proceeding which transpires between the FDA, and M-D Pharma, as well as the Education Concepts bunch. And we'll be happy to help with your preparation as such a witness."

A not-so-veiled offer, now clarifying the other offer which she'd just heard and 'couldn't refuse'. And what would Judith's 'staying in close contact' entail? And what might happen if she, now so well-informed, decided to decline their offer? So many questions to ponder.

"I will give this careful consideration, Senator Stanwood." She stood. He rose, as she continued, "I want to thank you again for all that you and Judith have done in this matter. And for the arrangements required to bring me here."

"You're most welcome. I've truly enjoyed meeting you, and hope this is the beginning of a long relationship."

Promising nothing, she said, "Thank you," and turned for the door.

He strode across his spacious office, and meeting her there, added, "You'd be a great asset."

"You flatter me," Rachel answered and turned to leave.

He stood in the doorway, hands in his pockets, totally relaxed in his element. "Well deserved, I'd say. Ms. Wilcox, would you bring me the Commerce Committee binder?"

Compartmentalized. Off to other business and the next set of issues.

Rachel's assigned agent pushed off the receptionist's desk and asked, "Ready?"

She noticed the enthralled young receptionist respond with a pout, which he answered with a wink.

Interrupting, Rachel declared, "Absolutely."

THIRTY-FOUR

May 2020

Sitting alone in her office, she scanned her desk. Two short piles left, then she could lock up and leave. The last three days had been rather intense, and fatiguing. She'd made more than several trips across town for meetings, secured hearings, and conferences with certain officials. Time to wind this up and head for the airport before anyone else sauntered in and laid claim to her time. She shuffled the piles, selecting a document which required her repeat review and signature.

Her assistant stuck her head in the door and said, "Ms. Quinn, ma'am, you have a call from Senator Stanwood's office."

"Thank you. I'll take it." Rachel put down her pen, picked up her phone, and swiveled her chair. Afternoon sun bathed the Capitol dome in warm light. Admittedly, her view was spectacular.

"Hello, Mark, how're you? Since we last spoke, what, two hours ago?"

"Rachel, thought I'd get back to you on that point you brought up at the meeting this morning…"

Question: would she get out of there after all? Her flight was scheduled to leave in three hours. She thumbed through the report as Stanwood's senior aide put words to his concerns.

~ ~ ~ ~

He stood at the baggage claim, waiting. MCI wasn't too busy that Thursday evening. Glancing at his watch, he realized it had only been five minutes since he'd previously checked. Arriving twenty minutes early had allowed time to tend to and delete numerous outdated emails, and to retrieve her flight update, which informed him it would be late due to weather—spring storms in the area. Impatient, he wished he'd waited longer at home. This arrangement of theirs was a bit tiresome at times, but he knew she enjoyed it, so he would strive to practice patience.

Carson whirled around at the sound of his name. Margo Hamm approached from a nearby gate, all smiles. "Hi, how's it going?" he asked. *That's right…she's been out of town all week.* He didn't keep his thumb on their legal department as much these days.

"Fine. A bit tired, glad to be home. And you?"

"Good, good. You were away this week in…"

"Dallas, on that case, you remember…the Southwest tech issue."

"Oh, yeah…how's that going?"

"Making progress." She redirected, "Waiting on someone?"

"Yeah. Rachel Quinn. You met her last fall."

"Oh, right. The drug company, the contract issue. How did that turn out?"

"You have a good memory…it's still meandering through several congressional committees."

"I'm not surprised. Sounds interesting. I'd like an update when you have time. Listen, I've got to run. My husband's at the curb. I'll catch up with you at the office, maybe next week." And off Margo went down the concourse and through a near door to her waiting husband.

Carson's cell buzzed. A text from Rachel. She'd finally landed, and they were taxiing to the gate. Shouldn't be long. He found a bench and sat. It *had* been an incredible seven months.

When he arrived earlier that evening, short-term parking had been sparsely occupied. As a result, he'd snagged an excellent spot. Now exiting the door together near baggage claim, they had an easy walk to the lot. They wove their way through a single row of cars to Carson's sedan.

He stopped before opening her door and drew her into a firm hug. "Missed you."

"I was only gone three days this time," she reminded him.

"Seems like more. How'd it go?"

Pulling back from his embrace, she said, "Busy. In other words, pretty much the same." She slid into the passenger seat, waited for him to take his place behind the wheel, then clarified, "A little progress on the contribution scandal, working its way through the House Oversight committee. The FDA's done gathering evidence on the data fraud. It appears they're close to a finish."

"Any hope it'll get resolved this year?" He fired up the car and backed out of the parking slot.

"Hard to say. It would be good if this gets done before the election, with the current committee chairs on board. And Stanwood is able, due to his position, to keep things in front of the right people. Still, it's a lot of slogging around, working with the aides, being patient with all the distractions they have to deal with."

Carson listened patiently to her venting. She looked exhausted, obviously in need of rest over the weekend.

"Tired? Want to stop for some food?"

"Yeah, I am. But no to the food. I ate in Chicago."

"All right. Let's see if we can beat the next storm home."

After paying his fee, he exited onto the main airport road. Approaching the access ramp to I-29, he sped up, merged onto the freeway, and beat a path south from the airport. They would need to cover thirty-eight or so miles to reach her place.

Thirty-Five

Curled up on the couch, Rachel nursed a cup of hot tea. Carson sat at the other end, legs stretched out, his feet tucked behind her. Subdued lamp light and soft background music eased her tension. Lightning flashed periodically, and rolls of thunder occasionally punctuated their conversation, a soothing sound for those accustomed to it. Spring in the Midwest, storm season.

Their discussion since arriving home had revolved around 'the arrangement'. He'd broached the subject, again. Traveling back and forth between Washington, D.C. and Kansas City had been exciting at first. She relished the challenge, but admitted the schedule had become a bit much. She'd never realized how demanding life in political circles could be. And it was obvious Carson wanted her to be home more, despite time he also spent with her in Washington.

"Have they placed you in another situation yet?"

"They've hinted, but haven't said anything directly to me."

"Judith hasn't mentioned it?"

"No. At least, not this week. You know, I hate to admit I enjoy infiltrating companies, insinuating myself into their hierarchy and figuring out what, if anything, is going on. The last two, though, were fairly straight forward, nothing out of joint. Rather boring, really. I told you about the one back in November, when we uncovered an active embezzlement scheme. Not exactly our purpose there, but it felt good to be of some assistance."

"Yeah, I remember you saying something about that."

"Frankly, working with several of the other politicians and their offices has been interesting. I've learned a lot. Getting to know them better and nurturing those relationships has given me opportunities I never thought I'd have. But we've talked about this before." She smiled, then paused, considering the serious expression he wore. "What's wrong, Carson? What's on your mind?"

"I don't know if I would say something's wrong, but I admit I'm growing tired of this routine."

"Tired of what you helped orchestrate?"

He gave her a long look and took hold of her hand. "Okay, we've gone over this before, too. I'll take my share of the blame. But I didn't make you say 'yes'."

"No, you didn't." She paused. "I don't assign blame to you or anyone. I've admitted I was angry, initially, when it was revealed to me how the whole M-D Pharma thing unfolded. How you came on the scene at just the right time. Acting so protective and concerned. I felt manipulated and deceived by several parties, including you."

Carson didn't argue. He couldn't.

"Not a good basis upon which to build a relationship," she added.

"No, it wasn't, I admit that."

"Truth is, at times I wondered why you were taking particular positions on specific situations, not getting too upset, putting off checking on certain details. Jumping all over something else. I thought it was just me being stressed, anxious, all that. To be honest, Josh suggested during one of our conversations that maybe I should question your motives. And I did, for about thirty seconds." She smiled. "Sitting with Judith and then Stanwood, I felt like a stupid fool. How easy I had been to use."

She went on, "Then, with the offer, my thinking transformed and I saw the advantages of the proposed position, felt persuaded by such excitement. I also rationalized that I was helping medicine, helping the industry, and the government with its tasks."

"That's a heavy load to carry. You were very good at what you did with that first case, which caught their attention. They need smart, level-headed people to step into those positions, people who aren't died-in-the-wool bureaucrats. You fit the bill then and you do now."

"I suppose you're right. But, you know, the whole scene is just plain seductive. Being in that environment, that super-charged atmosphere. I have to keep that in mind. Sometimes you don't want to leave. You want to baste in it. That's when you know you must get as far away as you can, and do something else."

"Are you considering leaving?"

"Oh, I've thought maybe I should get out of there. But, no, not yet, anyway. If I can keep that insight fresh, keep that governor on, then I think I'll be okay. I doubt this will be a permanent arrangement, not with the vicissitudes of politics. I like our situation as it is now, going back and forth." She regarded him. "Do you really hate it? You will tell me, won't you?"

"No, I don't *hate* it, but at times the commuting is tiresome, I admit. And, yes, I'll tell you if that day comes."

"Well, or if you see me slipping, please grab me."

"I won't do that, but I may sweep you away."

She squeezed his arm. "Sounds like a plan."

After a crash of thunder subsided, Carson asked, "You haven't mentioned the drug rep in a while. Whatever happened to Zera? Did she get fired?"

"She ended up in Dallas. Sometime in February, I think, I heard a tale about her and the national sales VP. Rumor was, they had a thing. When M-D Pharma came under the FDA hot light, he disappeared, and after that Zera took another position. I don't know the details. Judith only shared the basics to emphasize how the hammer came down on M-D, as well as how well the FDA was doing with their investigation."

"You didn't ever meet him?"

"No, I never did."

"I've wondered, occasionally, if that was him and her sitting outside the house down the street…the one for sale. You remember…?"

"Yeah, I've wondered, too, but haven't lost any sleep over the two of them. It was more important that the harassment stopped, and to find out we weren't really in danger with the feds watching."

"It sure didn't feel like nothing when I was wheeling around

D.C. with that agent. Maybe it was all orchestrated, all for show."

"You know, that's an intriguing thought. I wouldn't put it past them to plan something like that. I've never asked anyone about it, and doubt I'd get a straight answer if I did."

Carson paused and gazed at the windows on either side of the fireplace.

"Something wrong?"

"Not at all. I think the storm's let up. Why don't we call it a night?"

She smiled. "That sounds appealing."

An hour later, they lay entwined in her big bed, wide awake and satisfied. The storms had faded, moved east, only sporadically punctuating the quiet night with a distant roll of thunder. Carson had hoped for an opportune moment to broach the subject, and it seemed to have arrived. He turned on his side, gazing at her in the dim light of the darkened room, her hair a dark mass framing her face.

"You know what I've thought?"

"Probably lots of things," she answered, stroking his chest.

"Well, one thing in particular."

"Okay, and what is that?"

"I think it's about time we take the next step, make this legal."

Rachel pulled away and looked at him. She smiled. "Is that the most romantic way you have to propose marriage, if that's what you're doing?"

"I am."

"So, are you saying we're done figuring this out?"

"I am."

"Well, here's my not-so-romantic answer…I think I can cope with that."

EPILOGUE

January 2021

January is not the best time to visit Washington. Although typically devoid of tourist hordes, and for good reason, it is usually cold and often precipitating. But, not that day. It had dawned bright and sunny, cold but not windy. Now, if she could just take advantage of some of that sun, and avoid being relegated to the shade.

Rachel snugged the fur collar of her new red coat to her ears, her leather-gloved hands still warm. She absolutely was not going to wear a knit cap for this occasion, as much as common sense might dictate, nor earmuffs. No muffs. Despite the mid-calf length of her dress and coat ensemble, her hosed but otherwise bare legs, and sharp spiky heels felt dreadfully inadequate for the weather. Why hadn't she opted for slacks which matched her coat and sensible low heels? It would have been a much better option. But, no, not today. She envied Carson in his suit and topcoat.

They had stepped, in turn, through the large opening and out under the portico just fifteen minutes before, and had been directed to their seats by a uniformed young man. From their upper row, they enjoyed a great view of other guests as they were seated further down, some she recognized, others not. She caught a glimpse of Senator Stanwood and his wife. When he turned to scan the crowd, he spied them, nodded, and gave a brisk wave. They had come to be rather well-acquainted over the past six months.

What a truly amazing experience it was, in that place, at that time. Smiling, Carson reached over and gripped her hand.

Their view of the Mall was spectacular. Looking west toward the Washington Monument, and further beyond the Lincoln Memorial was, to say the least, inspiring. Not in her wildest dreams, while she watched, horrified, as Linda Bates writhed on her bathroom floor, could she have foreseen such an outcome to that situation. You just never know…

Not twenty minutes later, after the new Vice President was sworn in and the US Marine Band erupted in four *ruffles and flourishes* followed by *Hail Columbia,* noon arrived. She knew all this in advance, having studied up. Rachel watched as the newly elected President and his wife rose from their seats below them. Their two sons, now in their twenties, stood to the side. Unbelievable. With the First Lady holding a well-worn family bible and the Chief Justice standing opposite him, the President placed his left hand on the holy book and raised his right hand. Justice Roberts prompted him to recite the oath of office.

"I, Michael John Taggart, do solemnly swear that I will faithfully execute the Office of President of the United States, and will to the best of my ability, preserve, protect and defend the Constitution of the United States, so help me God."

Rachel smiled and squeezed Carson's hand. Yes, quite unbelievable, to say the least.

Author's Note

I wrote the original ADVERSE EVENTS manuscript in January 2020, before we realized a pandemic was upon us. But this story has nothing to do with that scrouge. While revising and preparing it for publication, I wrestled with those restrictions which would have changed characters and entire scenes. Instead, I opted to omit the pandemic as a factor, rather than contort the story to that dreadful period.

Interestingly, during revision another circumstance came to light—the concept of my fictional medication was realized. That is, research involving an osteoporosis medication being used to treat hand arthritis was reported at the *European Alliance of Associations for Rheumatology 2024 Annual Meeting*. My scenario, though, developed in the opposite direction—my fictional arthritis med could aid in the treatment of osteoporosis. Two truths emerge from this: one, the age-old question—does life imitate art or vice versa? And two, if you wait long enough to publish a story it may 'come true' in the meantime. Then someone believes you possessed foreknowledge, which you did not.

Let's remember, it's all fiction. These characters are not individuals I've known or treated during my practice years. And again, the scenes involving law enforcement or FBI characters are hopefully realistic enough to get a pass. If not, I accept all responsibility for any inaccuracies.

My editor Laura Taylor provided invaluable suggestions as she reviewed and critiqued the manuscript. Her insights and support are always greatly appreciated.

Kudos to Sharon Kizziah-Holmes for her expertise and patient assistance with manuscript formatting and preparation for publication. And to Jaycee DeLorenzo for collaboration on cover design, helping to shape my various, sometimes scattered, ideas into a cohesive design.

Finally, and always, I want to thank my husband for his steadfast encouragement. His perspective and consistent support through the vicissitudes of this process prove invaluable time and time again. I doubt this would be possible otherwise.

I enjoyed bringing these characters, their conflicts and relationships to the page. Hopefully, you found ADVERSE EVENTS a satisfying read, and I appreciate you sharing your time.

JJ Renck

March 2025

ABOUT THE AUTHOR

JJ Renek is the pen name of retired physician Dr. Janna Trombold.

Pivoting from a major in English literature, she pursued a career in obstetric nursing, and holds both a BSN and MSN in that field. A decade and two children later, she returned to medical school and received her M.D. from the University of Texas Southwestern Medical School in Dallas. During that time, she collaborated on several creative projects including faculty roasts and writing for the annual, irreverent senior video produced, in turn, by her medical school class.

Since retiring, she has penned eight medical suspense novels, and a collection of short stories across various genres. JJ makes her home with her husband, minus any wild pets, in the 'Show-Me State' where she writes full time, or pretends to.

You can follow JJ on Bookbub, Amazon, or Facebook at jjrenekauthor. Or to learn more about her and her books, visit her website at: www.jjrenek.com. While there, consider joining her newsletter group to receive regular updates and stay in the loop.

Made in the USA
Monee, IL
20 April 2025

3e886226-9133-479b-9525-05f8be97f417R01